FAVORED BY FELIX

SHELLEY MUNRO

MUNRO PRESS

First Munro Press electronic publication March 2017
First Munro Press print publication April 2025

DEDICATION

For Paul, my husband, partner in crime, and fellow adventurer. Every day is a good day.

INTRODUCTION

A new resort specializing in capture fantasies—the perfect place for Captain Casey Seonaid to blow off steam. To embrace her feminine side, possibly for the last time. And just as she'd hoped, it's not long before she finds herself "kidnapped". Let the sexual hijinks begin.

Attractive yet with an air of sadness, Casey snares Felix Mitchell's attention at first sight. As feelings deepen, he comes to realize Casey just may be his perfect mate. But despite their shared passion, something is amiss with his intriguing lover, something that keeps her from giving herself fully...something she won't share.

Unexpected troubles plague the resort, drawing the couple ever closer. But the biggest danger comes when Casey finally shares

SHELLEY MUNRO

her secret, revealing a familial enemy—and his shocking plans for Casey's future.

Inside Scoop: Felix may look big and bad, but Casey knows her shifter mate is just a big pussycat.

PRONUNCIATION GUIDE

Some of the alien characters within these pages bear Celtic names. Our heroine's surname is pronounced as follows:

Casey Seonaid: (kay + sea) shone + aid

CHAPTER ONE

C asey Seonaid wriggled and attempted to get comfortable. She flopped onto her side and prayed for the sweet oblivion of slumber. Seconds later, her body itched to move to a new position. *Scurvy sky pirates*, her brain buzzed like an angry drill-saw, too busy, too unsettled, too agitated to attempt sleep.

Finally giving up her valiant battle, she untwisted her body from the covers and slipped off her sleep-bed. She pulled on her robe—the garment she'd lovingly designed and made, rather than the complimentary resort one—and let herself out of the room she shared with her best friend Eva Henry.

At this time of the morn, the Middlemarch Resort on the island of Ione, planet Tiraq, was quiet—too silent—and jerked her from holiday mode into military.

Just what she wanted to avoid.

Sighing, she held her body still while she went through the

checks drummed into her by years of military training.

Look, watch, listen, smell.

Her glance proved she was alone. The long seconds she stood frozen confirmed nothing suspicious. Hearing check. Smell...

A slow smile curled over her lips. And she was back. The sweet fragrance of flowers, the close heat of the tropics, the faint tang from the waves running onto the shore scrubbed away the horrors of her job.

Automatically, Casey's feet turned in the direction of the sea. Bare feet, she realized, when she hit a gravel path. Too bad. She didn't intend to go back to their bungalow for something as pragmatic as footwear.

She limped over the gravel, another sigh gusting from her as she reached the more forgiving white sand. Her strides lengthened until she was almost running. As was usual, ever since her last meeting with General Seonaid.

Her father hadn't wanted a daughter.

He'd wanted sons.

Three sons.

And he sure as *phrull* didn't value her achievements or the way she'd advanced up the military ranks to match the careers of her two older brothers. No matter what she did, it wasn't sufficient.

She wasn't good enough for the general.

Casey slowed and padded across the white sand until she came to the edge of the water. A soft breeze wafted across her military-short hair and a wave washed over her feet. The water was cooler than she'd expected and startled a decidedly non-military *eep* from her throat.

"You shouldn't be out here alone," a male voice said.

Casey turned slowly, her leisurely action belying the way her heart drummed at her breast. Gods, she was more upset than she'd realized if someone could sneak up on her without raising her well-honed senses.

"Why not?" she asked, and openly studied the big man who'd emerged from the shadows. "The resort is in a fenced compound. The place is full of women." Lousy with them, the general would say. The thought brought Casey great satisfaction. "What could happen to me here?"

The man walked—no, prowled was a better description for his gait—closer and came to a halt a few feet from her. He flashed a grin full of white teeth, and she found herself returning the expression. A natural smile instead of the conscious ones she forced for her best friend while she pretended everything in her world was perfect.

"Let me see." He pretended to ponder while his gaze slid over her in a way that made her feel like a woman instead of a soldier. "I've heard there is a race of aliens who have a shortage of women. They're out to steal themselves mates."

"I'm all a-shiver," she said, returning his gaze of interest.

There was much to be admired. His black hair hit his shoulders and was three—*phrull*—*four or five* times longer than her own black locks. Even in the dim light cast by the astral moon and the resort's artificial illumination, she could see his gorgeous green eyes. Just a few shades darker than the color of the jade sea that surrounded Ione. His broad shoulders were garbed in a loose white shirt, his lower half in tight black trews and black boots, and he was taller than her six feet by a few inches.

"And what if I'm one of these alien males?" His voice held a smoky tone that reminded her of late nights and smooth aged liquor on ice. He stood close enough now for her to feel the heat coming off his solid body.

"I should start running?" Gods, was that flirtation? She'd thought she'd forgotten how since one didn't fraternize romantically with fellow soldiers. She cocked her head a fraction. "Scream for help?"

"You're lucky, sweetheart. Tonight, all I'm after is a kiss."

And he grasped her shoulders and pulled her to him, his mouth covering hers in a hungry kiss before she could gasp out a protest.

Sensations struck her like laser fire. His hot mouth. His hard body. His expertise. The pleasure of contact ripped away her lethargy. She gasped, and he took advantage, sliding his tongue into her mouth and stroking against hers.

So nice. So good. So perfect.

Casey gripped his shoulders and let his mouth ravage hers, blast her with the sensations she'd craved for long, lonely months.

Finally he lifted his head, grinned down at her while his thumb brushed across her tingling lips. "What's your name, sweetheart?"

"Casey."

"Felix," he said.

Her brows rose. "Not Alien Marauder?"

"Sexy Seducer."

Her brows inched a hairsbreadth higher, and she fought the burst of humor currently tickling her tongue for release. "You think you could seduce me?"

"Breathing elevated. Nipples hard. And if I was crass enough to check, I'd find you wet, or at least on the way there."

Common sense told her to knee him in the balls or punch his nose, but instead, amusement came to the fore, keeping the capable soldier at bay. "Rather sure of yourself, aren't you?"

"I haven't had any complaints." Those green eyes of his glittered in a silent dare.

"So are you going to capture me, tie me up and keep me as your slave?" A shiver went through her at the idea of being his prisoner, and she knew he caught the tell because his grin amped up into a full-on smirk.

Phrull, she must be more tired and stressed than she'd thought.

"You like the idea," he whispered, his breath warm against her cheek.

"Not really," she said dismissively, while her mind screamed *liar*.

Capture would solve her problems; put her out of reach of the general. *For a time.* He'd come for her eventually though, and toss her right back into reality—and turmoil—until her loyalty was tested to the limits. Gods!

"Let me kiss you again," he said.

"You're asking this time?"

"I figured that way I could progress to touching your tits, check if they feel as beautiful as they look."

Casey forced back the hysterical laughter battling for release. Now wasn't that a kicker? One of the offending body parts that made the general hate her was the very part this sexy man wanted to touch. She shrugged, fought angry tears and won. "Why not?"

Felix took her into his arms, pulled her tight to his body, and she discovered he wanted her. He liked what he saw. Heady stuff. She opened her mouth, let him use her as he wished and drifted on the pleasure of his hands on her body, drifted on the knowledge he wanted her, just drifted...because it was safer than concentrating on reality.

Or her future.

Felix Mitchell held the quivering woman in his arms, his curiosity roused. He'd watched her wander along the beach for the last couple of nights, wondered if she'd arranged to meet with one of the resort's male staff. Instead, she'd spent hours staring out to sea and looking so damn unhappy, she'd brought his protectiveness to the surface.

Most of the women who came to the resort wanted their fantasies brought to life.

Captures. Multiple lovers. Kink.

Whatever they wanted, Middlemarch Resort's male employees were happy to oblige, either in the virtual reality rooms or in a real scenario.

After the first time he'd seen her alone, Felix had started looking

SHELLEY MUNRO

for her during the day. She hung out with another woman—a petite blonde.

This woman—Casey Seonaid—and her friend Eva Henry had made the cut. He and his brothers intended to whisk them away from the resort and hold them captive until the women came around to the idea of staying. After much deliberation and weighing the pros and cons, he'd picked the blonde, Eva, as his potential mate.

Right now, he was starting to wonder if he hadn't made a mistake.

No matter which he chose, seizing a woman and running off with her was a hell of a way to find a mate.

Felix wasn't sure he approved. Hell, he didn't sanction kidnapping women and seducing them into marriage. Saber was out of his mind. Maybe losing his fiancée to the virus had done a number on his big brother's clever brain, and he'd lost his grip on reality.

But like his younger siblings—three brothers and a sister—he'd agreed with Saber and their mother that leaving a virus-stricken Earth for the unknown space frontier was preferable to dying. The rest of their evolving plan—the resort and the captures to replace the women who had died in triple the numbers of the males—he wasn't so sure.

Aw, fuck it. He'd talk to Saber, express his doubts again, *do* something for a change instead of merely resenting the way he worked and lived in big brother's long, tall shadow.

"I thought you intended to kiss me and touch my breasts." A faint tremor sped through her lithe body. "All you're doing is holding me."

"You don't like being held, sweetheart?"

"Doesn't happen very often."

Something in her tone had him pulling back to study her face. "Good or bad?"

"I don't need to be touched."

"Everyone needs physical contact." Felix pressed her head against his shoulder. For an instant, she held her body tight then she seemed to sag, her breath expelling in a sign of surrender. "My people—"

"Your people?"

"My family. We're very affectionate. Tactile. We like to touch. I especially like to stroke a beautiful woman."

"You're full of dino-crap."

He laughed at her blunt tone. She didn't pull her punches, didn't act like most of the hedonistic airheads who were staying at the resort. He and his brothers had chosen well. For a fleeting moment, he wondered if he should ask Leo to swap so he could capture this woman instead of the blonde.

No. He'd better leave things as they were. He'd snatch one last kiss before he left her alone. He lowered his head and claimed her lips. Started out slow, gentle, and then let the spark between them grab hold and flare hot and bright. His hand slid beneath the neckline of her robe to cup a heavy, naked breast.

She started before relaxing again. Her moan vibrated against his lips, and he decided to up the stakes. He tugged her nipple between finger and thumb, pulled another one of those sexy moans from her. His cock pressed against his trousers, his balls pulling tight to the point of pain so quickly, he felt dizzy. Fuck, this woman—she fired something in him.

Unable to resist, he lifted her off her feet and laid her on the sand, quickly following. He slipped his fingers inside her robe again, gave her nipple another twist, and she made a tiny mew at the back of her throat. Sexy. His hand smoothed over her stomach. He pulled at the silky fabric to bare her luscious body. Big breasts. Lean belly. Muscled frame with feminine softness, enough to entice any man.

Felix slipped his hand between her legs and found wet, hot flesh. He nudged her legs apart, half expecting a struggle, but she let him continue. Scalding honey made her folds slippery as he explored her flesh. He skimmed her clit, and she jolted.

On just the second pass of his finger, she came with a choked sob, the hard knot of nerves pulsing beneath his fingertip.

Felix smiled, kissed her gently and wished he had time to fuck her properly. But no, this woman belonged to his younger brother, even though she didn't know it yet. He'd already crossed a line when he kissed her and this finger fucking was doing a number on his guilt tripwire.

"Thank you, sweetheart," he whispered, and, unable to resist, kissed her one last time. He thrust his tongue into her mouth and smooched until he was desperate for a breath and had to lift his head. He traced her lips with his fingertip. "Maybe you can sleep now."

"Maybe," she said when he rolled away and stood.

She accepted his hand and rose before refastening the tie on her robe.

Unable to help himself, he brushed his fingers over her cheek and smiled down into her golden-brown eyes. "See you later."

"Bye."

And with a final wave, Felix walked away, even though every particle in his body urged him to forget—hell, ignore—Leo's claim on this woman and whisk her away to his rooms for a private capture.

CHAPTER TWO

"If your lady isn't in her bungalow, you'll find her on the beach. You'll probably be able to walk up to her without difficulty," Felix said.

Leo gave a curt nod, his mood terse and sullen. "Her files say she's military. I'm going prepared with a medi-cloth."

"Good idea." The tranquilizer cloths were useful. Felix opened his mouth to say more, to suggest a trade, but Leo turned away, fading into the darkness. He didn't know what was with his younger brother at the moment. Their mother was worried about Leo's unpredictable mood swings and recent weight loss, but when Saber had suggested he accede this first capture to one of the twins or one of their many cousins, Leo had lost it and struck out with his fists. Crazy times.

Felix shook his head and stealthily made his way to the bungalow Eva Henry shared with Casey. Time to get this show on the road.

"What's wrong, Felix?" Joe taunted. Joe was one of his younger brothers and came with a twin, Sly. *Identical* twins. They were identical pains in his ass and took great delight in teasing him. It was their job, they'd informed him on numerous occasions.

"Yeah, Felix," Sly said. "Did the little itty-bitty blonde get the better of you?"

His arm throbbed like a bitch where she'd bitten him and drawn blood like some storybook vampire. His ribs didn't feel so shit-hot either, where she'd used her pointy elbows to good effect. He wouldn't damn well underestimate her again.

If he ever had to do this again, he'd emulate Leo and use the medi-cloth straight away instead of as a last resort, as he'd done with Eva. Leo's capture was sleeping, and according to Joe, Leo had carried her off the beach in that state. Felix wasn't about to ask questions since Leo stood by the shuttle, a black scowl on his face. No doubt he'd be joking in a few minutes. Leo's black to white and back again mood swings made Felix dizzy.

Saber stalked up to him. "How is she?" Saber's eyes went right to the woman, her pale face and loose golden hair. His tender gaze as he stared at Eva gave Felix pause.

"Still sleeping due to the sedative on the medi-cloth," Felix said. "I'll wait around until she gains consciousness."

Leo appeared, with Joe and Sly trailing him.

Saber scowled. "How is the other woman?"

Leo lifted his hands in surrender. "Whatever the problem is—I didn't do it."

"Not guilty," Sly and Joe chorused.

Felix ignored his brothers and carried Eva past Saber. Sly and Joe took in Eva's form with undisguised interest, their gazes lingering on the woman's legs and breasts.

Saber issued a low warning growl.

Felix glanced back at his older brother quizzically, looking back and forth between him and the sleeping woman in his arms, before shrugging off the growl and continuing to one of the huts.

When he emerged, Saber was nowhere to be seen.

"He went for a run," Leo said.

Felix nodded. "Probably a good idea to scout the area. I'll check the fence to make sure nothing has broken through." Anything to take his mind off the way he'd hurt Eva. She'd have bruises, and she'd thumped her head. Fuck, he hadn't meant to injure her. He would tear off his left nut before intentionally wounding a woman.

The camp was a small clearing with two rough huts to one side. After they'd sighted several zylon in the region, he and his brothers had constructed a sturdy fence covered with fine mesh to keep the tiny furry beasties away from their captives. The last thing they needed was for their prospective mates to die of zylon poisoning. Bad publicity for the resort, for one; rumors of a horrid death would scare away prospective customers. These things had a way of getting out.

Felix paced the compound, taking his time, checking the fence for signs of zylon or any other nasties. The island of Ione reminded him of Singapore and Indonesia, although the land mass was much bigger than the two Earth tourist destinations.

When he found nothing unusual, he wandered back to where his brothers remained talking by the shuttles before abruptly changing direction. He'd better check on Eva. When he poked his head into the hut, she was still asleep and looked small and defenseless. He'd untied her upon arrival after he was certain the drugs had taken effect.

"Felix!" Saber must've returned.

He strode out of the hut. "Yeah?"

"I know why there aren't many zylon at this end of the island. I watched a bird catch one. A shit-ass big bird."

Felix chuckled, Saber's words reminding him of the vintage television shows they'd all watched as kids. "Was it yellow?"

"No, it was— Very amusing," Saber said. "How is the woman?"

Felix sobered. "I hurt her. I didn't mean to, but I hurt her. Saber, this is a stupid idea. Why don't we take the women back to the resort and forget the whole plan?"

"Fuck." Saber rubbed his hands over his face then stared at him. "We need mates to stop the fighting between our males. Damn it, Felix. We're sitting on a testosterone powder keg, and it's going to blow if I don't find a way to keep women here permanently. We need the stability that women provide. You know that."

"Things have already been calmer since the first guests arrived," Felix said.

"But they're not going to stay. We need mates, children. Strong family bonds. We've found a place to settle, but we have to make it into a home. And we have to do so while ensuring the resort's a success because we're running low on money."

Shock kicked Felix in the gut. He'd never seen his older brother looking this worried before. Almost desperate. "Why the hell didn't you say something?"

"I didn't want to worry you all. We can't stop now or we'll lose everything. I had to borrow money on Dalcon, the money we needed to get the resort running. I can't default on those loans. The trad-bankers weren't interested in financing me. I had to go to the market bankers. If the resort fails, if the males start fighting, our community will splinter. I *have* to keep us safe."

"Fuck," Felix said. "Those market guys don't muck around."

"Which is why we have to stick with the plan now that we've committed our resources."

"You *still* should have told us how bad our situation was."

"Everyone has been working so hard. I wanted to encourage them." Saber caught a flash of movement from the corner of his eye. An odd, rueful grin curved his lips. "Did you tie up your woman like I suggested?"

"No need. She was still unconscious," Felix said.

"She isn't now."

Felix turned in the direction Saber indicated. "Bloody hell. Where does she think she's going? We're in the middle of nowhere."

"She's a feisty one."

A shadow blotted out the sun-star. Felix scanned the sky. Saber cursed and started sprinting toward the woman. Without warning, a big-ass bird swooped, talons extended, and plucked the woman off the ground. Felix shouted, started running, his gaze darting from the bird and the woman to Saber.

Felix stumbled, cursed. Fuck. *Fuck.* He picked himself up and sprinted again. Saber put on a burst of speed and dived for the woman's legs.

The world seemed to slow as Saber grabbed her ankles, clinging tightly to the screaming woman and pulling. For an instant, the bird wavered.

"He's gonna do it," Felix muttered, partly in awe, urging Saber to maintain his grip. "*Come on.*"

For a moment it looked as if Saber's will would prevail—then the bird flapped its mighty wings and rose into the air, taking the woman *and* Saber with it.

Felix stood paralyzed as the bird raced through the sky, only moving when the beast flew out of sight. He raced for the shuttles. The twins were already in one, and Leo was waiting in the other. Felix hesitated in the doorway of the shuttle.

"Wait. Leo, we can't leave the other woman here on her own. She's your captive. Why don't you stay with her to make sure she's okay? Joe, Sly, and I will find Saber and Eva."

"No."

Felix blinked. "What? Why?"

"I don't want to do this," Leo snapped.

"But you agreed with Saber, said you'd take a captive for yourself."

"I lied," Leo snapped again, making Felix frown. Something was very wrong with his brother. "Look." Leo visibly calmed himself. "We're wasting time. You think someone should stay with the woman, *you* do it."

When Felix hesitated, Leo leaned over and shoved him in the middle of the chest. Felix toppled back and hit the ground. By the time he scrambled to his feet, Leo had the shuttle in the air and was heading in the same direction as the big bird.

"Fuck," he muttered then cringed at what seemed his new favorite word. His mother had been a dab hand with soap during his younger years, and she wasn't above rapping his knuckles now if she heard him or his brothers cursing.

He cast another glance at the jungle and prayed Saber and the woman got out of this alive.

A raucous *caw-caw* came from overhead and Felix instinctively dove for cover.

Another huge bird circled lazily then dived without warning. When the giant bird lifted back into the air, its talons clutched a hapless zylon. The zylon looked minute in comparison and not much of a meal for such a large bird. A snack, maybe.

After another wary glance at the sky, and with no intention of providing the main course, Felix climbed to his feet and trotted over to the hut where they'd left Casey Seonaid.

She lay on the bed, eyes closed, curled in a ball, her features soft and innocent. It made him realize how guarded she'd looked whenever he'd seen her around the resort. She'd appeared stressed, worried, as if a heavy burden weighted her down—apart from when he'd kissed her on the beach. Then she'd acted sassy and sexy and sweetly compliant—the perfect lover. It made him curious about her. Her life. He wanted to know more than the hard facts his sister Scarlett had uncovered during her research.

He kept thinking of that big-ass bird. How fast it had been. God, he hoped Saber managed to save himself and the woman. He shook his head. Nah, that was one thing he didn't need to worry about. Saber was resourceful. He'd save them. Felix was sure of it, and Leo and the twins weren't far behind in the shuttles. He took another look at the woman and left the hut.

Neither of the shuttles was in sight, and the sky was clear of birds.

Felix propped his butt on the edge of a rock and settled in to wait. Time passed slowly, and Felix checked on the woman again. She was still out. He hoped Leo hadn't given her too much tranq. He rubbed his hands over his face and paced back and forth in front of the hut.

Bloody hell, this first mate capture had turned into a hot mess that could splinter at any moment. Saber would be okay. He had to be. But if he were hurt, injured, then he'd step into Saber's shoes. He owed his brother to do his best and ensure everything worked as they'd planned.

Casey came awake; every one of her senses telling her something was wrong, out of place. She didn't open her eyes, didn't twitch so much as a muscle while she tried to recollect. She already knew she wasn't in the room at the resort. This one smelled different—kind of musty—and the bedcovers didn't hold the same floral scent. She cast her mind back, remembering, remembering.

She hadn't been able to sleep. *Again*. Despite being so tired she was acting like the walking dead species on planet Erastes. She'd gone for a walk on the beach while, for the hundredth time, attempting to decide what to do—carry out the general's wishes or disobey orders and lose everything.

"You don't know anything else. Besides, no one would dare touch you by the time I've finished."

As the general spoke, Casey recalled the expression on his face, one of triumph. Remembered the way her stomach had curdled because she'd seen that look before—right before he thrust his verbal sword and cut his opponent off at the knees.

"The vitamins your squad has been taking for improved physical performance help prepare your body for the technology. It's too late. The process has begun."

A low moan escaped her parched throat, and she finally opened her eyes. She struggled to sit up. Gods, where was she? While the bed was comfortable and the linen she was lying on clean and crisp, the walls were tree branches glued together with a reddish-colored mud. The ceiling of the hut consisted of a type of bright-pink plant. Someone had woven the leaves into a thick covering to keep out the solar light.

"Ah, you're awake," a cheerful male voice said.

It was him. The man she'd kissed on the beach. She struggled through the fog in her brain and came up with a name. "Felix."

"That's right, sweetheart."

"Where am I?"

"Captured," he said. "Enjoy the fantasy while you can."

Captured?

Of course! One of the resort's fantasy offerings. At least that would take her mind off her problems.

Felix's communicator buzzed. "Excuse me," he said and stepped out of the hut.

He must have stopped right outside the door because she could hear his side of the terse conversation.

"Get them? Fuck. They look okay? Yeah. Must be okay if they ran into the trees. Anywhere to land? Hell. That makes things difficult." An extra-long silence. "True. Come back here then. The twins can go back to the resort."

Casey frowned and viewed all four corners of the hut. This *wasn't* a virtual reality room? She'd thought... No.

Felix returned, his expression even happier than before.

"Good news?"

"Cautiously happy," he said. "I knew Saber would manage a miracle. He always does."

"Where are we?"

He shrugged, the faint movement of his powerful shoulders reminding her of his size. "It's not important. All you need to know is that you're here for the duration. My captive," he added with satisfaction.

Casey fought an unusual burst of humor and only just won the struggle to prevent a smile from sneaking onto her lips. "Sir, you can't do this to me. I'm an innocent and must get to my betrothed so we can marry on the morrow. You must let me go. You must."

"Huh?"

"Please, sir. I want to get married. My betrothed is a very rich man. He'll pay a rich ransom for my safe return."

"I don't want a ransom." Felix straightened, and insult dripped from every word.

Casey's brows rose. "No money? No jewels?"

Felix's brows squished together. "What are you blathering about?"

"Oh." She forced shocked surprise into her tone. "You intend to ravish me."

Felix rubbed his chin, studied her then flicked the sleep-bed a speculative glance. "I could deal with ravishment."

Oh, he was good. "But I must save myself for my future husband. I-I... Sir, is there anything else I could do instead? Maybe I could, um...touch you *there*?" She made a vague gesture in the direction of his groin.

"Later," he said, a faint twinkle in those sea-green eyes. "Are you

21

feeling all right?"

"A bit foggy in the brain."

"I'll get you something to eat and drink." He paused. "Am I going to need to tie you up or will you remain in this hut while I collect a meal for you?"

Casey glanced down at her hands and allowed her bottom lip to quiver. "I-I'll behave."

His expression took on an edge of suspicion, but he nodded and strode from the hut. Casey waited until she couldn't hear his footsteps and slid off the sleep-bed.

Scurvy sky pirates, what had happened to her? Her legs trembled, stubbornly refusing to take her weight, but finally, she pushed upright with the aid of the wall. She took slow breaths and tried to remember what had happened.

She'd been on the beach, walking. A noise. Yeah, she'd heard a noise behind her and thought it was Felix. It had been another man.

Scowling, she focused on pulling details from her quagmire mind. They rose from the murk, hazy and disordered. A pretty yet masculine face. What else? Her brow wrinkled when she came up with green. Yes, gorgeous green eyes a few shades lighter than Felix's. Heck, she had to be hallucinating. No man had such symmetrical features or long, dark lashes. Long hair.

The details emerged more quickly now. He hadn't smiled. No, anger had shimmered in his face, making those pretty eyes hard.

The man had grabbed her, and when she'd started to fight back, he'd held a medi-cloth over her nose.

The bastard had tranqed her with a sleep-drug. *Scurvy sky pirates*, now the fuzzy brain made sense.

Casey took a deep breath and attempted a couple of steps. She wobbled and remained upright. Better. Two more steps took her to the doorway of the hut. Her military responses came automatically. *Scout the location.* She scanned the area—a fenced enclosure—mentally putting together an escape plan if one became necessary. The fence was sturdy, but she could scale it easily enough.

A harsh *caw-caw* directed her gaze upward, and she felt her mouth drop open. *Rollicking reapers!* That was a freakishly big bird. She'd never seen one that enormous before, and she'd seen some weird sights while traveling with her unit.

She watched the bird swoop and come up with prey. The animal was still alive, and its terrified squeaks made the hair at the back of her neck prickle.

A shuttle came into sight and hovered over the treetops for an instant. The pilot landed the vehicle not far from a closed gateway. A man climbed out, and Felix went to meet him.

They didn't move far from the shuttle, which meant she'd have no shot at stealing the vehicle. Not that she *wanted* to escape, not when she could fool around with Felix. *Anything* to escape her bloody thoughts and the dilemma the general had forced on her shoulders.

Her happiness faded. Her mouth firmed.

"Decide. Yes or no. It's a simple decision."

Simple for *him*.

Casey swallowed and decided to test security for her amusement because she sorely needed some fun and joy in her life. A distraction.

She slipped from the hut and cursed the dirty robe she wore. It was light in color, the same shade of moonlight as her nightgown. While it was a great garment—one of her own creations, so it was well-designed and comfortable, as well as sexy—the color would stand out against the bright pinks and blues and the mottled greens of the plants and trees. Oh well. It wasn't as if she was trying to escape. She was getting what she'd paid for, after all—a capture fantasy.

When she crept closer to the transport, sticking near the fence and taking care with foot placement, she saw the two men looked alike. The man from her hazy memories stood with Felix, arguing. *Planetary zombies*, her memory had underplayed his prettiness. The man was gorgeous, despite what appeared to be a high temper, yet no one could call him feminine. He was all male with his hard body, black hair and gorgeous face.

She turned her attention to Felix. Some woman might not give him a second look after seeing the first man, but she liked the slightly coarser features, the grin that was a fraction lopsided. If a woman hooked up with the pretty one, they'd always have to watch their backs in case another woman tried to steal him away.

The two men continued to argue until the pretty one let rip with a punch. It caught Felix unaware, and he went down. Pretty man turned his back and stomped to the shuttle. Seconds later, the vehicle fired up and rose into the sky. Casey remained frozen in place, but she watched the departure of the shuttle until it disappeared over the treetops.

Interesting.

She studied Felix and watched him climb to his feet. Cautiously, he worked his jaw back and forth and let out a grunt that carried across the compound.

Casey did a rapid visual sweep of the area, including the sky, and crept away, putting distance between herself and Felix but keeping him in view.

This was a fantasy, and it was her job to act like a ninny and try to escape. Every good capture contained drama.

Felix went into the second hut and, after a few minutes, came out with a tray. He walked into the other building. Seconds later, she heard his curse and grinned. The instant he emerged, she'd let him see her and take off. He'd catch her, she knew, because she didn't have footwear, and the surface appeared rough and uneven.

Casey checked for birds and other types of possible danger, then saw Felix appear and took in his panicked expression before she stepped into view.

Then she was off, tearing across the pink and green grass, chortling as she ran, glorying in the exercise and the chase.

This was so much fun! She didn't know why she hadn't booked into a resort like this before. She kept running and was halfway across the compound before footsteps thudded behind her. She increased her pace, surprised when she ran faster than ever before. Her feet tangled, brain shorting at the realization, reality pressing down on her psyche.

Seconds later, he tackled her, and she went down hard. Before she could yelp at the dig of a rock in her ribs, he rolled to his feet, plucked her off the ground, and hurried toward the hut.

Once inside, he dumped her on the bed and locked the door. Her heart knocked against her rib cage, rapid beats that held a trace of dread. She stared up at him, saw the flare of his nostrils, and quivered.

His eyes were hard. His mouth pulled to a firm line, and his hands clenched at his sides. He prowled to the edge of the bed. "Are you hurt? I want to make sure you're all right." He removed her robe and inspected her hands and arms, her legs, and the soles of her feet.

"Take off the nightgown." He left no room for doubt. This was an order meant to be obeyed.

"I..." Casey paused, traces of uncertainty unfurling inside her mind. Had she pushed him too far?

His hand flashed out, and he grasped the neckline of her nightgown. She froze, her gaze snapping to his stormy one.

"Not fast enough," he purred and gave a mighty tug.

The rent of the fabric filled the hut as he tore her nightgown from bodice to hem, and shocked, she just blinked.

The tiny matching panties drew his gaze. "Off," he said.

Casey remained rigid with shock. She hadn't thought...hadn't expected this level of reality with her fantasy.

Felix gave a half grin and grasped her panties before she could move. He tugged them down her legs in one smooth yank and deposited them on the floor. He lifted a light and held it over her nude body.

"You've hurt yourself."

Casey gave her body a quick visual sweep and prodded a bright-red spot. "Just a bruise."

"You've cut your feet. They'll need treatment. Wounds go septic quickly in this heat."

Casey stared at him, now totally confused. Then her mind cleared. Of course. It wouldn't look good for the resort if the guests were injured.

Felix picked up an urn of water and pulled a basin from beneath the sleep-bed. He reached under again and came up with a small med-box.

"Sit on the edge of the bed."

When she followed his order, he didn't peruse her naked breasts or ogle the rest of her body, and a trace of pique filled her. Instead, Felix pushed the basin closer and half-filled it with water. She studied his face as he tended to the cuts and nicks one foot at a time. He produced a towel and dried her feet before spraying on anti-germ. The serum stung, and she bit her bottom lip because the way he showed such concern made her want to bawl.

Soldiers don't cry. Soldiers don't cry.

The stern words she'd heard since childhood echoed through her brain.

Soldiers also followed orders—and she hadn't. Unknowingly, she might have sabotaged the general's plans because she hadn't liked the taste of the new vitamins or the weird way they made her feel. Right now, Casey wasn't sure if that was a lucky break or not.

Regardless, if the general got his way, it likely wouldn't make a *phrullin'* difference.

Gods, she was losing her mind. A male showed her a bit of

kindness and it turned her inside out.

"Okay?"

Casey swallowed, nodded, not wanting to risk speech because those tears were hovering like that big bird, waiting for an opportunity to swoop.

"Good." Felix tidied up and set the basin of water aside. Then he turned to her and roared, "What the fuck did you think you were doing? It's dangerous out there! You can't just wander around on your own."

Casey blinked, shock keeping her quiet. No one ever worried about her safety. No one showed concern. No one did anything except give orders and expect her to complete missions. "Ah...sorry?" she said, a faint query in her voice.

"You're sorry?" he snapped. "Gods, if anything had happened to you—" He broke off and dropped onto the edge of the sleep-bed. "Come here."

Puzzlement drew her brows together, and she knew he saw her confusion.

"I don't ever want to go through that again," he said, his voice soft yet more powerful for the leashed emotions.

She eyed him warily as he patted his knee.

"You didn't think I'd let you get away with scaring me half to death, not without punishment."

Again the soft voice, the scary tone that made her hesitate.

"Casey." He patted his knee again, and this time it was very clear what he expected.

Casey vacillated a fraction longer before edging closer.

"That's right, sweetheart. Drape yourself over my knee."

When she faltered again, he pounced, grasping her upper arms and dragging her over his knee. One second, she was staring into his jade eyes, and the next, she stared at the dirt floor.

Her legs scissored, arms flailing in an attempt to get free. Felix held her in place without difficulty, his hand a heavy weight in the middle of her back. Finally she subsided, lying quietly over his knee, her heart pumping anxiety through her body.

The crack of his hand against her bottom dragged a pained cry from deep in her throat. She squirmed and wriggled, kicked her legs once more, but he controlled her struggles and smacked her again. Hot, angry heat reverberated across her skin. Pain pushed at her stupid tear ducts again, and this time, a tear rolled down her cheek.

"You will not." *Smack.* "Do anything." *Smack.* "So foolhardy again." *Smack. Smack. Smack.*

Another tear plopped to the ground. Her flesh burned where he struck, and each smack landed in a different place, agitating a different part of her bottom.

"Do you hear me, Casey?" This in a silky tone, one she hadn't heard before. "Casey?" His hand roughly caressed her burning buttocks, and she winced. "Are you going to answer me?"

"I hear you."

"Good girl." He lifted his hand and smacked her again.

She cried out, her shout cutting off abruptly when, this time, his hand settled on her buttocks and stroked rather than punished. A heat of a different kind blossomed between her legs. Her breath caught while her pulse raced.

"But to make sure you think hard before disobeying me again, I'm going to give you two more blows. That will be ten in total. Do you agree with your punishment?"

"No."

He chuckled, a rich sound that intrigued her. Unwillingly. The man was a bossy brute.

"Too bad," he purred. "Because I rather like the look of my marks on your pert ass. I like the fiery color on your cheeks." His fingers stroked and delved, made a foray between her legs. "And I think secretly, you might like it too." *Smack.*

No doubt about it. This time the heat had a decided sexual edge, and desire directed her blood downward to pulse in her pussy.

"Do you agree?"

"No."

"Liar," he purred, and as if to prove his words, he struck another blow, the angle different. Lower.

A lick of heat roared through her, and this time, she felt her arousal fully and heard the sound of her excitement when he slid his finger along her folds. He skimmed with skill and purpose, teasing her clit while holding her in place.

"Imagine my cock filling you," he said. "Sliding inside your moist flesh until I'm balls-deep. Can you imagine that?"

A shudder went through Casey as his words seemed to crawl inside her and take root. Gods, she wanted a man that way. A real man, not one of those pleasure droids she had to make do with whenever her squad had leave. She wanted—no, *craved*—a real flesh-and-blood man like Felix.

His finger moved, lightly massaged, and a thrill of pleasure streaked from his touch. The movement of his digit came to a stop, and she felt the pulse of her clit, the way it swelled at his touch.

"Imagine me sucking your nipples until they change color from light pink to cherry red. Each time I suck, you feel it down here." He pressed her clit, and it jumped beneath his touch. "Then think about me fucking you hard, cramming inside your pussy so deep we'll feel as one. We'll both come, and once we've taken everything each of us has to give, we'll smell like each other. Any other male will know you belong to me."

Her heart jumped at his words, even though she knew he didn't mean them. This was a game. Pure fantasy. But oh, she liked the sound of it—the raunchy fun. The sense of knowing he wanted to mark her with his scent. So primitive and thrilling.

"No comment?" His finger moved again, a sensual slip and slide. Then he thrust a finger inside her, grunting with satisfaction.

She cried out in protest when he withdrew his finger, her hips jerking as she tried to drive him deeper. The hot skin of her backside pulled, the streak of pain combining with the erotic teasing of his finger to make something better.

"It's all right, sweetheart," he crooned and drove three fingers into her needy flesh.

Casey gasped at the intrusion. It wasn't painful. In fact, it was just what she wanted, and she made a hum of pleasure when he set up a quick rhythm. On each withdrawal he twisted his fingers, catching a sensitive spot deep inside her. A groan sounded and his laugh told her the throaty cry had spilled from her mouth. Gods, that felt good.

"Do you like the feel of my fingers, Casey?"

"Y-yes." Her body shuddered when he hit the special place again.

"Can you imagine my cock? Can you imagine my body draped over yours as I slam into you from behind?"

"Yes." Gods, she wanted that so much.

His fingers thrust, pulled out, thrust, pulled out. She quivered, her hips rising and falling on his lap as she strained to reach the climax hovering on her horizon.

His fingers danced over her delicate flesh. They teased, and Casey squeezed her eyes shut. Her heart was hammering so hard she wondered if it might climb up her throat and burst from her mouth. Felix moved his fingers, stroked, and she came so hard she saw stars. Her channel pulsed around his digits, clutching and releasing for long moments until the spasms tailed off.

"Good girl," he whispered, and pulled his fingers from her body.

He lifted her off his knee and placed her facedown on the bed. "Stay," he said when she attempted to roll over. "Let me put something on your backside to take away the heat."

Too bemused by his actions and wrung out from the orgasm, she gave up the idea of disobeying because it seemed like too much effort to fight.

"This will feel cool," he warned. "But it'll take some of the residual sting away."

She started, despite his warning, the cold salve a shock against her hot skin. And he was right—the ointment did take away the heat.

He shifted off the sleep-bed and she turned her head, curious as to what he was doing now.

Stripping.

His boots thudded onto the dirt floor then he started working on his shirt. One fastening at a time popped open. Her breath caught upon seeing his bare chest, the bulge of muscles as he shrugged off his shirt. Muscles more spectacular than anything she'd imagined when they were together on the resort beach. The corners of his eyes crinkled, and she felt an answering grin knock against her lips, ready to come out to play. He knew she was interested. *Scurvy sky pirates*, she was more than interested. Man-deprived soldier that she was.

His hands dropped to the fastening of his trews. She watched, enthralled, as he revealed more of his body. His hips, his muscular thighs and long legs, and when he straightened, she got her first glimpse of his cock.

His erect cock.

"Like what you see?"

Her tongue swiped across her bottom lip, and her gaze skipped up to his face to find him grinning.

"Casey? Are you going to answer?"

"Yes. I haven't had sex for so long. Don't tease me."

Interest glinted in his eyes. "How long?"

"Whenever we have furlough, we stop at one of the pleasure planets. Only droids available there. No men."

"So you haven't had sex with a *real* man for how long?"

"I can't remember." And she never would if the general had anything to do with it.

"What about the men on your squad?"

"It creates problems within the squad. Discipline. Jealousy. Envy. Problems with the chain of command. Sex screws everything up."

Felix nodded and cupped his cock. "Understandable." He stroked himself, his gaze on her the entire time.

Casey licked her lips again, and he gave a soft groan.

"I'm not going to go easy on you this first time, Casey."

"That's okay." The truth was, even though she'd come and climaxed hard already, she ached to feel his cock stretching her. And even more, she craved the feel of him wrapped around her...because no one touched her anymore. "You won't hurt me."

Weirdly, she truly believed he wouldn't hurt her. She didn't know why—it was a gut instinct, and in her line of work, that aptitude was part of the skill set.

Felix released his cock and crawled onto the sleep-bed. He pulled her into his arms, and she shivered at the avalanche of emotions that struck her with brute force. Foremost was the sense of connection, and tears—those wretched tears—stung her eyes again.

Why? Why did she have to find this man now when it was too late and everything was about to change?

CHAPTER THREE

F elix stilled at the sudden tension in her body. "Have you changed your mind?"

"No!" She gripped his shoulders with talon-like fingers. "No, I want this. You."

Instead of answering, Felix pushed her flat on the mattress and rose over her. With his thigh, he wedged her legs farther apart and settled into the space he'd created. Her arms wound around his neck, and she gave a sigh—a happy one, he hoped. Something he'd said or done had tripped her buttons and caused unhappiness to cloud her whiskey-brown eyes.

Felix lowered his head and pressed a kiss to her temple. Her hair was prickly beneath his exploring fingers. So short. He usually liked his women with long hair.

"Why do you keep your hair so short?"

"So I blend. It's important to fit in with the military style of life."

She sounded as if she was regurgitating an oft-repeated lesson, her tone rigid like the volcanic stones littering the compound.

"It feels spiky yet soft. Smells good too. I bet the other soldiers don't smell like you."

Her nose wrinkled, and some of the murkiness disappeared from her eyes. "No. Some consider it a point of honor to shun the sanitary unit whenever possible."

"I bet they spruce up before they hit the pleasure planets."

Casey made a scoffing sound. "Of course they do. They want to get lucky with the real thing, if possible. Too much talking." She drew his head down to crush their mouths together.

Since she was heading in the direction he wanted, Felix allowed the distraction. But the important thing was he knew she'd used sex to change the subject, and his gut told him it was something in her military life causing her heartache. He could be patient. He had days to exert his fortitude.

Felix settled in to erase her problems—for a time, at least.

He took the kiss deeper, made it slower, more suggestive until his balls burned with the need for release. His hands plucked at her breasts and tugged on the pink nipples until the color deepened to a pleasing rose.

She was with him every second of the way, her hands roaming his back and his buttocks, meeting every kiss with urgency. Her soft cries pushed at his feline. Felix gritted his teeth, astonished when he felt his canines lengthening.

Crap! He'd never faced this problem before. *Double crap!* His claws were starting to protrude from above his fingernails.

Faster. He needed to stop with the lazy exploration and getting-to-know-her stuff. "Close your eyes," he ordered. "Tell me everything you're feeling."

"I feel wonderful," she said with a happy sigh. "My breasts are tingling, and I can feel myself getting wetter and wetter. Ready for your cock."

"Pleased to hear it." God, his voice. It sounded as if his throat were full of gravel. Time to get moving with this fucking. The last thing he wanted right now was to show her his dual nature. Bad enough that he intended to keep her, possibly against her will. One shock at a time would work best.

Felix ran a careful finger down her slit and found she hadn't exaggerated her readiness.

"*Ooh*," she said and shivered.

That did it. Felix guided his cock to her opening and slammed home with one seamless thrust. Balls-deep, he panted, trying to get a firmer grip on his feline.

"Move," Casey ordered.

Felix chuckled and obeyed her bossy tone. He withdrew and thrust back hard. She winced, and he froze. "Am I hurting you?"

"My butt's sore," she whispered, and a delicate pink flooded her cheeks.

"I didn't know soldiers blushed."

"I don't. We don't." At the mention of the military, she went wooden beneath him, and he silently cursed.

"The sore bottom will help remind you that misbehaving won't go unpunished." Unable to stop himself, he pulled back and plunged into her moist heat. Her sheath clenched around his cock, gripping his dick in a loving embrace. Fuck that felt good, made him wonder why he'd waited so long to have a woman.

"Faster, Felix."

"Whatever the lady wants." He set up a fast pace of thrust and withdraw, his balls screaming at him to release, but he gritted his teeth, foolishly wanting to come with his new mate. He wanted perfect for their first time. He squeezed his fingers between their bodies and stroked her clit. The tiny bundle of nerves was swollen, much to his relief. He gave her a couple more rubs, and when he felt the ripple of her channel, he pulled back and let himself go. One stroke. Two. Three.

She groaned, and the spasms around his cock became more regular. He stroked into her one more time, and his orgasm exploded like a volcano. Sensations tore up his dick, and streaked through his body until he felt as if he were imploding. The contractions of his cock went on for long moments before tailing off and ceasing.

"Wow," Casey said. "That was worth waiting for."

That would be a hell yeah. Felix shifted his weight so he wouldn't crush her but remained inside her body, liking the physical contact. At least neither of them needed to worry about producing offspring from their mating. Saber had insisted his brothers get control inoculations, and women visiting the resort had to consent to receiving a similar common shot upon arrival. No messy slipups for Middlemarch Resort. The control inoculations made things simple, and spontaneity would never hit them over the head with consequences.

His feline had settled, but Felix felt him beneath his skin, the contented purring. They were both in agreement.

Casey Seonaid was the one for them. She would become their mate.

Casey woke hours later, after the best sleep she'd had for weeks. Felix was stretched out beside her, soft snoring sounds coming from him. It was kind of cute, and it allowed her the freedom to visually explore his body.

Coming from the military, she was used to muscular men who kept in good shape. Felix certainly didn't fail on that score, and she couldn't wait to tell her best friend Eva about the spectacular sex.

The best friend she might never see again after this trip.

The unhappy notion slipped to the fore as she thought of the general's plans. She wondered if her mother had known of his perfidy, then scowled. Of course, her mother knew. Her mother grasped everything the general did and presented a united front with her husband even if she disagreed with his actions. The picture of a good military wife.

Wife.

Phrull. They'd given her screeds of documentation about the process and told her to read everything before she asked questions. So far, she couldn't bring herself to open the folder. It was locked in her briefcase back at Middlemarch Resort. But now she wondered about children. She'd never consciously thought of the possibility, but now...

If she decided to go along with the general's plans and opened that briefcase—

No! Tears stung the back of her eyeballs, and she swallowed hard. Why not admit the truth to herself, at least? She hated the general's plan and was appalled at the lengths he'd gone to to achieve his goals. She was more than a commodity, *phrull* it. She was his daughter.

His daughter.

The urgent need to scream her fury pummeled her, and she scrambled off the sleep-bed. She was halfway across the dirt floor before she recalled Felix. Glancing back, she noted her abrupt movements hadn't woken him. Casey stumbled to the door, opened it, and bolted outside. Rapid footsteps took her to the middle of the compound and she let rip with an unearthly howl of anguish.

The chatter of birds came to an abrupt halt. The hum of insects ceased as her frustrated screams rang out again and again and again.

Felix appeared in front of her. His face—his mouth was moving. He was talking, but she couldn't hear anything above the shrieks. The anguished cries that ripped up her throat and exploded outward.

His hands curled around her shoulders, and he shook her.

Another scream rippled through the air. And another. Another. Another...

Her throat burned in protest, the interior raw, stinging, each new scream shredding a path of pain. Her head throbbed in concert, but she couldn't seem to stop.

Felix shook her again, then drew her into his arms and hugged her hard, almost squeezing the breath out of her. She started to hear him, could just make out the words above the desolation swamping her mind.

"Casey, sweetheart. It's all right. Everything is going to be all right." His hand smoothed down her back, a reassuring stroke. His voice was a low murmur, and the urge to scream gradually receded.

Instead, tears overflowed her eyes in a never-ending stream, shrouding her vision.

Soldiers don't cry. Soldiers don't cry.

For once, she didn't give a flying *phrull* about soldiers. She wanted to be plain Casey Seonaid, the woman who liked sewing and fashion and spending time with her likeminded aunt but kept it hidden because such *female* interests weren't worthy hobbies.

Felix eased her away and studied her face. "Sweetheart, did I hurt you?"

She shook her head, swallowed, winced. At least she'd stopped crying. Probably dehydrated and her body didn't have any water to spare. She stared at his chest and saw the dampness caused by her tears.

"Then what's wrong?"

She'd been mistaken. Her body had plenty of tears left, and they trickled from her eyes anew, no matter how much she blinked.

"It's nothing I've done?"

She shook her head again.

"Okay," he said, tenderly brushing a tear off her cheek. "It's not safe out here. We'll go back to the hut and tuck you into bed. Then we'll have something to eat and drink. Have you ever tasted Earth wine? I stole a bottle from my brother's stash. He'll try to kick my ass, but it'll be worth the beating."

Casey let Felix guide her back to the hut and put her to bed, this time with the covers over her naked body. *Phrull*, she'd run outside with not a stitch of clothing. She was losing it. The military doctors would have fun dissecting that one, and she could imagine the general's disgust at her weakness, her older brothers' ragging.

Maybe she should have stopped in to visit Aunt Elsa, her mother's younger sister, before she'd left Dalcon. She'd wanted to, but self-preservation had kept her away. Elsa would have seen something was bothering her, and would have pried and meddled to discover the truth.

Casey turned her face into her pillow and let it absorb her unhappiness. Running away wasn't helping, but she wasn't sure she had the strength to stand against the general.

Not alone.

Most people who had parents and siblings went *to* them if they had trouble, to discuss and sort out their problems.

Not her.

The general's ambitions *were* her problem, and her mother, her brothers, never went against the general. The man was a law unto himself, both feared and revered by her peers.

Phrull, no matter which way she looked at the problem, she was screwed.

Felix selected items from the food stash he'd organized and placed them on a tray. When he'd heard her scream, he'd panicked. Thought one of those big-ass birds had snatched her, or worse, a cute and fluffy zylon had enticed her to pet it before the creature sank poisonous fangs into her silky flesh.

She wasn't crazy—he sensed that with every particle of his gut—but something big was ridin' her hard, causing her all kinds of mental and emotional stress. She obviously didn't want to talk about her problem. Frustrating as hell, not knowing what the obstacle was because he wanted to be there for her in every way. He wanted to fix stuff and make things right.

No, the best thing would be to give her space but plenty of affection and loving. He could almost hear his mother giving him the advice, so he knew his gut instinct was right. Hopefully, in time, she'd come to trust him.

He grabbed the bottle of wine plus the two fancy glasses he'd pilfered from the bar and added them to the tray. Wine plus snacks to entice her to eat and some harmless conversation. Yeah, sounded like a plan.

When he entered the hut, she was exactly where he'd left her, but he could tell she wasn't asleep.

"Casey, you have to try this wine. This bottle comes from our own vineyards back on Earth. It's a sauvignon blanc. I want you to tell me what fruity notes you pick up from your first taste."

She rolled over in the bed and he got his first glimpse of her face. It was pale and blotchy from her weeping, the lack of color highlighting the shadows under her eyes caused by sleepless nights. His heart twisted hard, but he bit back words of concern. *Distract her. Chatter about nothings.*

"Here, you take a sip while I sort you out some food." He gave her face another quick glance and noted her thinness. He added more cheese to the plate and a fruity pie. Whatever was worrying her had possibly led to weight loss, as well as emotional trauma. He prayed the food didn't hurt her throat too much. He placed some of the local fruit on the plate—soft, pink, juicy, and easy to digest.

After snatching up his glass of wine and the plate of food, he went to her. "What do you think?"

"I went to Earth once. That's where you're from, right?"

Her voice emerged throaty, and it sounded as if it hurt when she talked. "Yeah. We left because of the virus. We lost a lot of friends and relatives during the outbreak. They say the population loss was even greater than the black plague of several centuries earlier."

When she looked blank, he grinned. "Old Earth history. You were saying about the wine?"

"I tried a fruit there. Peaches?"

"Close," he said, letting his approval show. "Definitely hints of stone fruit. I'd say it was more nectarine than peach or maybe apricot. Do you like it?"

She nodded and took another sip.

"Have some fruit."

She took some, but he could tell she didn't really want it. She was placating him. Following orders. He frowned. Why didn't she tell him no?

Because she instinctively followed commands.

Felix reached for a cracker and cut a slice of cheese to place on top. He bit into it, his gaze still on Casey.

The sound of a shuttle returning had him rising. "I need to speak with my brothers."

Instead of demanding to go back to the resort, she nodded in a lethargic manner.

Felix quashed a second scowl and stalked out to meet Joe and Sly, his younger twin brothers. Hopefully they had more news about Saber and Eva. Leo hadn't said much. "Did you get them?"

"No," Sly said.

He and Joe slid out of their shuttle and joined him.

"We saw them," Joe said. "They escaped the bird."

"They were bloody lucky," Sly added. "Another bird appeared and attacked. The two birds were squabbling over which one got Saber and the woman."

"Fuck," Felix said. "Did they look injured?"

Joe gave a curt shake of his head. "The first bird dropped them. I saw Saber drag the woman into the jungle where the birds couldn't get them, so they're okay."

"I tried to get Saber on his com," Felix said. "It's turned off."

"We tried the com too," Joe said. "Hope it didn't fall out of his pocket."

"Did Leo come back?" Sly asked.

"Yeah. He was in a hell of a mood," Felix said.

Joe's brows drew together. "Still?"

"What bug crawled up his ass?" Sly demanded.

"Hell if I know," Felix said. "He's been moody and biting everyone's heads off since we left Dalcon."

"Maybe he's tired. He worked long hours on Dalcon and has returned several times to finish a job." Joe shrugged. "Who knows with Leo."

"Do you want us to stay?" Sly asked.

Felix wasn't sure what was best. Maybe he should take Casey back to the resort and get his mother to look at her, maybe dose her with some vitamins, and he could make sure she ate properly and slept. He'd tire her out with sex, if necessary. She didn't seem to have a problem with him touching her.

His com-unit buzzed in his pocket, and Felix glanced at the screen, some of the tension leaching from his shoulders. "It's Saber. Saber, you guys all right?"

"Yeah. A bit banged up and a few bruises. Listen, I need you to return to the resort and ensure everything goes okay. Go through the next lot of guests with Scarlett and work out a list of potential captures." Saber continued, running through the items that needed attention.

Felix listened to Saber's terse instructions. "What about you? Don't you want us to come and collect you?"

"No. Eva booked a capture experience, and that's what she's getting. I hope you don't mind if I do it instead of you."

"No, that's fine." Relief straightened his shoulders. He could keep Casey with him and pamper her until she regained her balance. No point telling Saber that Leo had pulled out and he'd decided to take his brother's place. "Call me if there's anything else you need or if you think of anything you've missed."

"Anything comes up, you take care of it," Saber said. "I'm going to turn my com off. I don't want it ringing at an inconvenient time." He clicked off abruptly.

Felix returned his com-circle to his pocket. "Saber said he's staying with the woman and intends to keep her."

Joe let out a long whistle. "That's interesting."

"What about Lori?" Sly frowned at his brothers. "Or Laurence, come to that. Laurence won't like it if he thinks Saber is replacing his sister."

Laurence wasn't rational about his dislike of Saber on a good day. Back on Earth, Felix had suspected Lori and Laurence wanted a slice of the Mitchell empire, but now—now the coffers were bone dry, according to Saber, and still Laurence hung around. Hell, maybe he'd been wrong about the money being Lori's chief interest. Saber had clearly loved her even if Felix hadn't thought much of the woman or her brother.

Everything had changed since they'd left Earth to escape the virus. They'd kept their capture program quiet, deciding to try it with family members before they offered other Middlemarch males the same opportunity. Saber had said it was a chance to perfect their process, and this way, they wouldn't raise hope or jealousy. At least that was the plan, and they'd all gone along with Saber, even though a couple of them—particularly, him and Leo—had reservations.

"I hope Saber knows what he's doing," Joe said. "We haven't had time to explore much of the island. God knows what else is out there. Those big-ass birds have to eat *something*. I'd just as soon they didn't decide to come to the resort side of the island and put us on the menu."

"He has his com-circle. We can go and pick him up the minute he sends word," Felix said. "Do you mind going back to the resort and returning to pick us up tomorrow? I'll clean up the huts and be ready to leave in the morning. That'll give us a chance to get to know each other."

"She could leave you once she's back at the resort." Joe said what Felix was thinking, worrying about.

"I know. That's why I'd like another night alone with her before we head back. Saber has given me a list of things to deal with, but one night won't make any difference."

"Tomorrow morning then," Sly said. "I'll com you before I arrive. I don't want to hurt my eyes or besmirch my innocence by witnessing any kinky goings-on."

Felix snorted and waved his cackling brothers away. He hid his smile until he turned his back and strode back to the hut. It was good to have brothers, even though they were a pain in his ass at times. He at least understood Laurence's grief at Lori's death because losing any of his brothers would send him into a tailspin.

He found Casey holding her wineglass and staring into the swirling contents. Wherever her mind had drifted, it wasn't a happy place.

"Hey, you haven't eaten."

"I'm not hungry."

"Try to eat something," he urged, taking a seat on the corner of the bed. "I want to jump you again before we go to sleep, have more hot, kinky sex. You need to keep your energy up."

Her gaze zapped to his. "Again?"

"You're very attractive. I like you."

She lifted a self-conscious hand to her hair. "I look like a boy."

"You don't *feel* like a boy. If you don't like your hair the way it is, change it. Grow it long. You should do whatever makes you happy."

Casey bit back her snort with difficulty. He made it sound easy, but he'd never come up against the general's indomitable will. She'd grown up with the man and found her life went more smoothly if she went in the direction he pushed.

But not this time, her mind screamed.

Not. This. Time.

If she went against him, she'd lose everything. Everyone except maybe her Aunt Elsa. She sighed, knowing her time was ticking away. Two more days before she left the resort and walked into the medical center.

Two more days.

The thought mocked her, shoved fear through her veins, and not for the first time she told herself she didn't want to do this, no matter what arguments the general pushed at her.

"Why the big sigh?"

"Maybe I'm hungry after all." She caught the flicker of disappointment in his eyes before he turned away to cut her a piece of what looked like pie.

When he handed her the treat, she bit back a wave of nausea, but she forced herself to take a bite rather than make a liar of herself.

"What do you like to do when you're on leave?" Felix asked.

Casey swallowed. She had a family-approved life, which meant she attended concerts and went to formal dinners or parties...and she had her secret life where she slipped away to meet her aunt. They visited the fabric market and went to fashion shows—with Casey in disguise, of course. It wouldn't do to let the general know she was "misbehaving". And she spent long hours indulging her creative self, designing outfits and stitching elegant designs.

"Casey?"

She lifted her chin and took a deep breath. "I visit with my best friend, Eva. We go shopping in the market, and I like to design clothes then stitch them."

Interest, rather than polite dismissal, glinted in his eyes, and some of the tightness faded from her chest.

"Are you any good? My sister Scarlett was complaining that there are few decent designers on Dalcon. Would she have seen your work?"

Her tension ratcheted right back up. "No. I don't have time to do much designing these days. Work gets in the way." She swallowed, needing to rid her throat of the cold, hard knot that had grown to the size of her fist. Soon, work would take over completely. She'd become a pet project and would never have the life she—

No point whining about it now. No point at all.

"I used to go surfing a lot when we lived on Earth," Felix said. "I haven't had a chance to try it here."

"I don't know what that is."

"You have a fiberglass board and float on it, allowing the waves to propel the board forward. The trick is managing to stay upright without falling off. I'll take you sometime. The waves farther down the coast from the resort look big enough."

That tightness clamped her chest, making it difficult to breathe. Her eyes stung at his casual kindness. He hardly knew her and would never see her again after she left Middlemarch Resort. But she didn't say anything, managed a creditable nod.

"Do you see your family much?"

"D-depends where I'm stationed. Sometimes, my squad does training exercises with my brothers' units. My father—he's a general. I see him on lots of training vids, and occasionally, he'll stop by the posts where my brothers and I are stationed."

"Did you always want to be in the military?"

"I never considered anything else." Because she knew what a shit-storm stepping off the Seonaid path would bring. It was easier to follow orders and keep her head down. *Scurvy pirates*, maybe she should have fought expectations from the start. Looking back, that might have made a difference.

When the mental pain threatened to overwhelm her again, she asked, "What about you?" She barely forced the words out before the knot crammed her throat shut.

"Me?" He pulled a face. "I fit in where my oldest brother thinks I'm needed. I'm a competent farmer, have a good nose for wine, and appear to have a talent for all things mechanical, which has kept me busy at the resort."

Casey gave a hard swallow, curious despite her misery. "Do you resent your brother?"

"Sometimes. Saber makes everything look easy. He heads the family and sorts out our problems. He won this resort in a card game, saved us from wandering. Gave us a place to set down roots. Fuck, I sound as if I'm jealous of my brother."

"It's hard when you have older brothers who are good at everything." This time the words came easier.

"Yeah." Felix laughed. "They cast a long shadow. Eat your pie and drink your wine. Promise me you'll try to eat more food. I don't want your beautiful breasts to fade away. I'm going to do one last perimeter check and sort out the other hut. The shuttle is coming back for us early in the morning."

Casey stared at Felix and forced her lips into something she hoped resembled a smile. It must have worked because he skimmed his fingers over her cheek and stood, leaving the hut without a backward glance.

Those tears burned her eyes again, the knot in her throat grew to unbearable proportions and she struggled to breathe. Despite that, a laugh squeezed free—bitter and savagely amused.

In two days, the general expected her to report to the military hospital, where he'd booked her in for nanotechnology.

By the end of the week, she wouldn't have breasts at all—because she'd be a man, with all the working equipment of one.

The perfect Seonaid soldier.

CHAPTER FOUR

C asey managed to eat a little, but her throat hurt and her head thumped in concert with her heartbeat. Too many messy emotions rattling her brain and heaping on top of the fatigue from long nights of tortuous thoughts.

Felix came inside and shut the door, bolting it for the evening. The glimpse she got of the compound told her night had fallen in the rapid way of this planet. One moment it was light and the next, the sky became inky black.

"Do you have sexual fantasies?"

His blunt question came out of nowhere, especially since she was expecting praise for eating, as he'd directed. She blinked.

"I put capture on my form," she said. "Do you have headache tablets in your med-box?"

Instant concern leaped onto his face. "You're not feeling well?"

"My throat is sore, and my head is pounding."

"I'll get you something. Get into bed. You look as if you could do with some sleep too. Maybe we'll postpone the sex until tomorrow morning."

A protest escaped her before her sluggish brain overrode the verbal tell, and he sent her a rakish grin. *Pretty when he smiles full-out.* At least she'd have this weekend to remember. No, wait. Hadn't she heard the nanos would shuffle her personality and memories, take away any female traits or thoughts? Once she entered the clinic, she wouldn't remember Felix and how he'd made her feel.

Alive.

Beautiful.

Feminine.

And above all, desirable.

"Here, take these for your head." Felix handed her two tablets. "And one of these for your throat." He handed her a solid lump the size of a fingernail. "Let it dissolve in your mouth and it should soothe your throat."

"What is it?"

"Nothing sinister. My mother makes a lot of our medical supplies. They contain natural ingredients. Once we get back to the resort, Ma can take a look at your throat and make you something else to soothe it."

Casey tried to imagine her own mother carrying out such a domestic task and failed. Her mother went shopping, had lunch with the other military wives—the ones with husbands of rank—and organized perfect parties and balls. Her mother kept busy with her social life.

After cleaning up the food and other things they'd used, he stripped and slid into the sleep-bed beside her. He reached for her and pulled her into his arms, pressing her face against his chest. At first, her body remained tense, but gradually, his warmth permeated her muscles, and she relaxed. His presence eased her constant obsessing about her shortcomings, her limitations, her failings—the ones listed by the general during their last meeting.

Felix made her feel safe.

He lowered his head and kissed her lazily, sipping from her mouth, tempting her to participate. Sweet warmth, like the syrup Aunt Elsa poured on her honeycakes, slipped through her veins. He kept up the gentle kissing, treating her like something precious and fragile. The idea—that someone thought her worthy of such care—made her stomach whoosh but in a good way. His fingers and hands stroked and caressed, teased and tempted until her muscles became malleable, like a piece of silk cloth. He nipped her breast, the sharp teeth pushing pain through her. The sensation startled her, yet it grabbed hold of her senses made the syrup in her veins, the heat in her pussy, take on a tinge of dark need.

She wanted him. Gods, how she wanted him to permeate her body, overload her senses until she could no longer think but only feel, feel, feel the pleasure and wallow in the bliss.

He seemed to understand because he rolled her under him, parted her legs, and pushed inside her willing flesh. The first thrust filled her, gave her what she craved. She ceased thinking about her unpalatable future. Instead, she left herself drift, let Felix direct their bodies, and clutched his shoulders to enjoy every pleasurable sensation. The way his cock filled her so beautifully. The musky scent of him. The way he kept kissing her and rasping his tongue over and around her sensitive nipples.

"Do you like the feel of me inside you, Casey?"

"Yes."

"I can't get enough of you, enough of this," he whispered in a deep voice right next to her ear. "I'd fuck you all night if I could and fall asleep still joined with you."

Gods, he said the sweetest things, made her yearn for the impossible. A life away from the military. A life like Eva's, where she could do what she wanted, when she wanted, instead of following orders and more orders.

Felix halted his thrusts. He lifted his head so he could see her eyes. A flash of something—maybe anger—darkened his gaze. "Where have you gone? Your body has gone stiff. I can feel your mind has wandered. Do you want me to spank you again?"

A jolt speared her stomach. Definitely a sexual one. "I'm sorry. I'll try harder." And she would. It was her fault if the general intruded and spoiled this slice of paradise. She promised herself she'd relax, drive the general out of her head. Shove him to the door and lock his robust, military-fit butt in a mental dungeon.

For the hell of it, Casey pictured herself forcibly removing the general. A chuckle emerged.

"You think a spanking is funny? It won't feel very good on top of the one I gave you earlier." He smoothed a firm hand over her buttocks, and she couldn't prevent her wince.

"When I'm with you, I want to your focus. Understood?"

"Yes s—" Casey broke off with another wince. Military conditioning had her responding to the order before she'd even thought about the action.

"Yes, what?" he prompted.

"Yes sir." The response fit better when it was directed at Felix. She *wanted* to obey him. Strange. Did that mean she'd always followed her work orders under protest? Something to consider. The general's plans had required her retirement from service. Officially, she was no longer military...

Felix withdrew from her body then entered her again, this time with force behind the thrust. He went hard and fast, changing the angle until he hit her in the perfect spot with every plunge. She moaned, raked her fingers down his back, lifted into his strokes.

"Felix!"

"Casey." He twisted his hips, drove deep, and she whimpered. When he pulled right out of her without warning, she groaned a protest.

"What—"

Before she could finish her question, he turned her on the bed and lifted her body so she balanced on her hands and knees, her head hanging low and confusion filling her. Then Felix crouched behind her, ran his hand over her buttocks then slipped it between her legs to play with her heated flesh. He thumbed her clit and sent jolts of pleasure through her. She clenched her butt muscles, wanting to hold the wonderful sensations, the heat and the excitement of his attentions.

The anticipation.

He pushed a finger—no, *two* fingers inside her core, but that didn't dissipate the desire trembling within her, the sensual fire flickering through her veins. "Felix, please. I need your cock inside me, filling me. Please."

"As the lady desires," he purred. "And since that's what I want too..." He drifted off, the pause a meaningful one filled with promise.

She felt him position himself behind her, felt the prod of his cock and then he was sliding deeply into her body. Her sheath fluttered at the rasp of intrusion. She gasped and rocked back, driving him deeper still. So good, so damn good, especially when he curled his chest over her back.

He whispered a rush of hot, erotic words against the rim of her ear. "You feel amazing. Hot and wet. Tight." His mouth latched onto her neck, and his tongue darted out, rough and slightly abrasive against her sensitive skin. All the time his hard flesh invaded her, and her stomach went fluttery, a coil of pleasure building, building, building.

She was wet with want now, her stomach muscles clenched tight as she shuddered and shook, lost in a sensual haze.

His hands roamed her body, he nipped her neck again—and a burst of heat and pressure rampaged through her.

It became too much, not enough. She writhed against him,

a fine sheen of sweat coating her body. He gripped her firmly, his fingernails digging into her to the point of pain, driving her. *Driving her.*

Then the tension detonated into an explosion that made her breath catch before emerging with a cry of delight.

"Felix!" Casey sobbed out his name as she came around his cock.

It seemed to be the signal he was waiting for because he slammed into her even harder than before. He roared out her name and collapsed on top of her, his heart pounding against her back at an impossibly fast pace. For an instant he stilled, then he separated their bodies, leaving her bereft.

Tears sprang to eyes that had watered like taps all day. Should be used to it—the physical rejection, being alone. As squadron leader, her work was solitary until a mission, when it was her job to make sure everything went according to plan. Then it was back to being alone again, isolated because of her position. *Scurvy space pirates,* she should be used to emotional segregation.

Her earlier panic returned in a giant wave. Not good enough. She couldn't be, otherwise the general wouldn't want to change her. Give her an "upgrade".

Not good enough. Not good enough.

"Hey, why the frown?" Felix tugged her back into his arms and covered them both with a blanket.

A tremor of relief slid through her, so strong she barely restrained a groan to go with the shiver, and she clutched his shoulders, burrowed against his chest and soaked up his warmth. A man who didn't know her at all showed her more caring, more tenderness than her family had ever given her—apart from her aunt.

She pressed a kiss to Felix's chest, needing to show her gratitude. She couldn't tell him anything, not when he was a stranger, but hopefully, if she succumbed to parental pressure—as she knew she would—she would remember the one man who'd treated her kindly, had made her feel worthy.

A second kiss escaped her lips and hit him to the right of his nipple.

"Sleep now, sweetheart. We have a busy day tomorrow."

They did? Her eyes fluttered closed, and she let herself drift on the cloud of contentment that came with being in Felix's arms.

Best capture fantasy ever.

The shuttle landed in the compound not long after daybreak. Felix strode toward the vehicle and was surprised to see the twins inside.

"I thought Leo was going to collect us," he said.

"He left for Dalcon to pick up supplies for Ma," Joe said.

"Well, as long as someone came to pick us up."

"Where's the woman?" Sly asked, humor dancing in his green eyes. "Did you tire her out or has she run off screaming into the jungle?"

"Very funny," Felix muttered, yet he felt too loose and limber to put any punch into his reply.

"Ma sent some clothes for her," Joe said and handed over a bag. "Scarlett donated them, although she wasn't very happy. Said she didn't have many to spare."

"Thanks, I'll buy Scarlett something nice next time we go to Dalcon."

"Do you want anything loaded into the shuttle?" Joe asked.

"The boxes in the first hut. We won't be long," Felix said.

In the hut, Casey was still asleep. Felix watched her for long seconds, loath to wake her when she needed the rest. He'd let her sleep late tomorrow—after he explained he had no intention of letting her board the shuttle back to Dalcon. Lucky for him, his private suite possessed stout locks on the door. He had a feeling he'd need them.

"Casey, it's time to go. Casey..."

She bolted upright in the bed, eyes wide and her hair sticking up in short spikes that reminded him of a ruffled hedgehog. "Is it time to ship out? *Phrull*, why didn't my alarm go off?" Her head shook from side to side and her eyes focused, narrowed a fraction.

Fascinating to witness—the transition from confusion to full alertness. Felix smiled and handed her the bag. "My sister Scarlett sent you some clothes. Why don't you have a quick wash and change while I pack up here? There's cold water in the basin over there."

Something slammed shut in her expression. An unpleasant thought? Felix didn't know, but it made him ache to hold her, and he went with instinct. "They say on my planet if you exchange a kiss in the morning, the feel-good factor increases a person's life by five years."

"I don't believe you." Hard, clipped words. Military words.

"But a kiss is such a simple thing, an exchange of affection. Why would you risk the rapid passing of years if you could slow them with a kiss?" This time, he pounced, grasping her shoulders and tipping up her chin for easy access to her mouth. He took the kiss, used his expertise to urge her to respond, and after a long hesitation, she settled her hands on his shoulders and leaned into him.

Felix wanted to cheer. Instead, aware of his brothers waiting, he pulled back and pressed a brief kiss to her forehead. He lifted her off the bed and stood her on her feet. "Joe and Sly are here to take us back to the resort."

She gave a curt nod and retreated to the basin of water, grabbing the soap and towel he'd left for her use.

Felix started to strip the bed because Ma would kick his butt if he didn't leave the place clean and ready for the next series of captures.

Casey...Casey was a puzzle, one he intended to solve. The sad and forlorn expression he caught on her face twisted his heart and poked at him. He wanted to take her into his arms and tell her that whatever worried her, he'd take care of it. He'd take care of *her*. Silly, since he'd known her mere days, but she spoke to the warrior in him, made him want to protect, to become a better man...to become *her* man.

Instinct told him to wait, to let her come to trust him and confide her secrets when she was ready, but patience didn't sit comfortably on his shoulders. His feline didn't like the idea of waiting. Felix grunted as he worked. Never had he been so aware of his feline pulsing under his skin. Oh, he was conscious of his dual nature, but since meeting Casey, his feline struggled for control. Or was it his imagination? Damn if he knew.

Maybe he'd shift later tonight, ask his brothers or Scarlett if they'd like to go for a run. They could hunt for zylon, and make sure the population around the resort remained low.

"I'm ready."

Felix turned and almost choked on his tongue. In deference to the tropical heat, Scarlett had sent a pair of brief shorts that showed off Casey's long, lean legs and a tight T-shirt in a hot pink to rival the surrounding vegetation. The words *Mega Babe* were emblazoned on the front across her breasts.

"You look gorgeous," he said.

She tugged at the hem of the short T-shirt. "I don't usually show this much skin."

"You should," he said. "Let's go."

She picked up the bag and a box without being asked and followed Felix from the hut.

A piercing wolf-whistle rang out, echoed by a second one.

"Eyes off," Felix snapped. "You're here to transport us home, not to ogle my woman."

"But the scenery is so pretty," Joe said with a wink.

Felix checked Casey's reaction and found her blushing,

although her eyes were wide and brought to mind a startled child. Had she never experienced flirtation? Maybe not, considering her father, the general, and her career path to squad leader. Perhaps he'd let the twins continue to flirt with her.

He gritted his teeth and ignored the mental snarl of his feline.

"Let me help you into the shuttle, Casey," Sly said and rushed forward to take the bag and box. "Here, Joe." He thrust them at his twin. "Stow these, will ya?"

Joe muttered a low curse, and Felix smothered a grin as he gathered the last supplies.

The shuttle ride took longer than Casey expected, although she hadn't been conscious on the outward journey. The jungle they flew over was thick and vibrant with color.

"Fuck, there's one of those big birds over to the right," Joe said.

Casey peered out the window and saw the bird soaring toward them. The wingspan was incredible, bigger than any bird she'd ever seen.

"It's heading straight for us," Felix said in a tight voice.

"Don't worry," Joe said. "I think we'll be more maneuverable."

Scurvy space pirates. The bird was going to attack. Fear slid into Casey, jacked her pulse rate and set adrenaline charging through her veins.

Felix reached for her hand. "Steady, sweetheart. Joe is a top-notch pilot."

"He really is," Sly said with pride. "Lucky *he's* flying and not me."

"Do these birds come near the resort?" Casey asked in a faint voice. The bird was so close now she could make out the hook of its beak and the glint of the predator in its beady eyes.

Joe shifted the path of the shuttle, and the bird adjusted accordingly. Casey curled her fingers around Felix's, thought of dying, crashing in a huge fireball because of a bird. Imagine that. The general would fall into one of his famous rages, where he threw the nearest thing—object or hapless aide—at the wall or the floor and stomped out his anger at not getting his way.

A laugh ripped from deep in her chest, taking her by surprise.

"That's the spirit," Sly said, his hands racing across the weapon controls. "We're gonna send this bird back to its ma."

"You okay?" Felix murmured.

She squeezed his hand. Surprisingly, she was fine. If she died, she did so with her own memories, and the man she'd come to like and respect would be at her side.

"I'm gonna fly close to give you a killing shot, so get ready," Joe said. "Fire!"

The entire shuttle shuddered and dropped hard and fast. Casey's stomach duplicated the move, and she let out a cry of alarm.

"There's another fuckin' bird behind us," Sly said. "Fuck it. I missed."

"Damage report," Felix demanded.

"Our surveillance equipment is off," Joe said. "Otherwise, we're in good shape."

Their calm acceptance of the situation went a long way toward jerking Casey back into military status. "I'll watch out this window," she said.

"I'll watch this side," Felix said.

"Coming in fast from your right," Casey said.

Joe put the shuttle into a steep climb. "First bird ahead," he said.

"On it," Sly said and fired. Once. Twice.

The shuttle bucked. The bird issued an eerie shriek, its giant wings faltering.

"Shot," Joe said.

"Second bird now coming in from the left," Felix warned.

Joe made the shuttle drop rapidly.

"I see it," Sly said.

"Fire," Joe snapped.

Sly fired, and the bird screamed. It paused, hovering in front of the shuttle before swooping downward and away.

"What happened to the other bird?" Felix asked. "Do you see it, Casey?"

"Not on my side."

Joe zipped upward and turned the shuttle. "I see it. Ahead at one o'clock. It's retreating. Wow, that was a trip. Let's get *our* bird home."

Casey relaxed and sank back into her seat.

Felix laid his hand on her knee. "Good job. I'm glad you're not a wimpy female."

"I second that," Sly said. "We wouldn't have escaped as easily if you hadn't kept your cool."

Praise. It washed over her like a gentle balm. She *had* done a good job. She always did, but it was kind of sad that it took three strangers to recognize her expertise.

"I'll check out the shuttle once we get back to the resort," Felix said. "All the gauges are right?"

Joe scanned the instrument panel. "Yeah, apart from the rear surveillance cameras. They've gone black."

Casey went back to watching the passing scenery while the three brothers chatted to one another about various things to do around the resort.

In the distance, a plume of dark-purple smoke rose from a conical-shaped hill. The occasional opening showed in the treetops, but mostly the jungle appeared thick and difficult to penetrate. She'd traveled through terrain like that before and didn't have fond memories of the experience. Not only had she lost a man, but the entire squad had suffered from a foreign rash that itched like the blazes for weeks after returning to base.

Finally, their shuttle touched down.

"Home sweet home," Joe said.

"We're going to have to wait until Saber gets back to get the approval to plant the vines," Sly said.

Vines? Casey started paying attention to the conversation.

"You two are responsible for the farming side. If you think conditions are right for planting, I say go for it," Felix said. "You want me to take a look? Tell you what I think?"

"Yeah, that would be great," Joe said. "Can you do it before you start working on the shuttle?"

Casey intercepted Felix's quick look at her. "I'm curious about what you're talking about. Take me too."

Felix relaxed his shoulders and shot her a blinding smile filled with approval. In a daze, she climbed out of the shuttle and followed Felix and his brothers from the landing zone. They strode past a huge shed, its yawning double doors letting her gawk at the pieces of machinery and tools, most foreign to her, and toward an open area. The soil was turned and loose and ready for planting.

Felix crouched and scooped up a handful of soil. "Looks good. How did the tests come out?"

"Better than the home vineyard," Joe said, and Casey heard the excitement in his voice. She listened as the three men discussed technical stuff that made not a jot of sense to her, watched the animation on their faces and couldn't help but see the obvious affection between the brothers. It was difficult not to contrast her family life—not that they ever spent much time together—and the way they were all expected to confer with the general. The general had always made the decisions and *still* expected to make them for his adult children. Once a Seonaid, always a Seonaid.

Some of the good mood, the calmness she'd claimed since Felix had wrapped her in his arms last night, started to dissipate. The hard-fought-for tranquility sank through her toes and into the ground beneath her feet.

"Casey?"

Her head jerked up, and she realized she must have made a sound.

"What is it, sweetheart?"

"Nothing." But it wasn't nothing. It was everything, and the entire mass of hurt and pain threatened to pull her under and squeeze the air from her lungs.

"I'll get you back to the resort," Felix said, slipping his arm around her trembling shoulders. "I think you should plant the vines now, guys. Conditions are optimum. Besides, Casey likes our wine. We'll need to have more to refill our cellar."

Casey let Felix guide her to the resort, her mind dwelling on his words. The future. He spoke as if they'd see each other, know each other.

She didn't have a future.

Unless...unless she stood up to the general and said no. The idea sent spurts of panic pumping through her, hard enough to make her tremble.

She'd tried to say no before and had attempted to exert her independence. Memories of dark cupboards and no meals. The disappearance of her pet furbie.

"You don't look well, sweetheart," Felix said. "I don't like the way you keep shivering, and you look exhausted. I'll get Ma to take a look at you. She'll know what to do."

Casey nodded since he seemed to expect some kind of reassurance in exchange for his concern. She let him guide her past a busy kitchen and down a long corridor. Finally they came to an open courtyard. The same lush tropical plants in vivid pinks and blues that filled the resort were planted here, with a few green trees with copper-colored trunks to cast shade. A pale-pink fountain, shiny in the solar sun, made a tinkling sound and somewhere a bird sang a sweet, melodious song.

Felix knocked on a door.

"Ma," he said when the door opened. "This is Casey. She's not feeling very well. Can you take a look at her?"

The woman was tall with dark hair elaborately arranged on top of her head, and she possessed gray eyes, not green ones like her sons. Lines fanned around her eyes when she smiled and stood aside to let them enter.

"My son," she said. "She is very pretty. Come, my dear." She took Casey's hand and tugged her to a seating area. It was nothing like her mother's immaculate rooms, done in an endless sea of white with syn-chrome accents. This room was a riot of color, blues and greens with splashes of turquoise and crimson, yet it seemed to marry together into a peaceful and comfortable abode. A spicy scent permeated the air and the low notes of a song came from the corner, a male voice crooning along with the music.

Casey let the woman push her down on a couch.

"Let me get some refreshments," she said. "Have you heard from Saber?"

"Not since last night. He said he was fine."

"I know," the woman said. "Saber is very resourceful, but I worry. It's a mother's job."

Felix laughed and gave the woman an affectionate cuddle before she pulled away with a throaty chuckle and hurried from the room.

He'd *hugged* his mother. She'd been *worried*.

"Something wrong?" Felix asked, taking a seat beside her. Although there was plenty of room, he crowded against her and slipped an arm around her shoulders, as if he couldn't resist the physical contact.

"My mother never hugs me. I can't remember—" She broke off, aghast at the admission. She was forbidden from discussing her parents or brothers with anyone, except in the most general terms.

"Never?"

"No." Her reply sounded small. Ashamed.

He took her hand in his and squeezed in silent commiseration. "I'll make up for it. I promise." And his eyes glowed with a brighter jade green as he sealed his promise with a kiss.

CHAPTER FIVE

"**I**'m worried about her, Ma."

Felix sat with his mother later that night. Casey was in his bed a few doors down, fast asleep, her slumber aided by one of his mother's special tonics.

"She's underweight and looks exhausted. I don't think it's anything more serious than stress. I think she's come to the point where something is worrying her so much, it's affecting her physically."

"So what do I do? I'm keeping her, Ma. I like her a lot. She's feisty yet vulnerable and makes me want to look after her."

"How's the sex?"

"Ma! I'm not telling you that."

A burst of humor showed in her gray eyes. "Can't be much wrong in that department then. I knew I brought you and your brothers up right."

"You have done a stellar job, Ma." Felix paused, considered. "No, nothing wrong there. In fact, she seems more relaxed after sex. It's the in-between times that are a problem."

"When she has time to stew," Anna Mitchell said. "The more I hear, the more I think this is a classic case of stress. She'll need lots of rest and relaxation, plenty of one-on-one time from you. She needs to fill her time with things she enjoys doing—maybe a hobby of some kind."

"She likes to sew," Felix said, after thinking hard. "She mentioned something about doing her own designs."

"Perfect. Scarlett and I were discussing opening a shop that caters to our female guests. Clothes, maybe jewels and beauty products. We think it will be another revenue stream. Maybe she'd like to help?"

Felix nodded, his mind busily prodding for disadvantages to the idea. He couldn't see any.

"Why don't I ask Scarlett to drag her off tomorrow morning? It will keep her busy. Scarlett won't let anything happen to her," Anna said.

"Thanks. At the moment, she still thinks she's catching the shuttle home tomorrow. I might have to lock her up if she objects."

"Don't worry, son. I've seen her watch you. She likes you, so it may not be as difficult as you think."

"I hope so." His communicator squawked at him and he absently picked it up to answer. "Yeah?"

"It's Saber. I can't talk for long. Any problems?"

"Everything is fine." No need to tell Saber about the bird attack or the damage to the shuttle. The vines. He'd dealt with it, and if Saber didn't like his decisions, too bad. "Do you want to talk to Ma?"

"Not now. Just wanted you to know we're about four or five days out from the resort, I think. Depends on the terrain. I might not get a chance to call again but don't panic. Gotta go," he said.

"Saber," Felix said to his mother. "He said he'll be another four days at least before he gets home."

"I hope everything is going well. Saber needs someone after Lori. I never thought that girl was right for him." She paused. "Don't you dare repeat that to anyone."

"I won't. I'd better check on Casey before I head to the workshop."

"The remedy I gave her should keep her out until the morning. She needs sleep. She'll feel much better for it. I'll talk to Scarlett for you, and we'll put our plan into action. It will be nice to have the opinion of another woman. Sometimes, I think Scarlett's head stays in her technological equipment, and she answers me on automatic. I can't be sure her opinion is objective."

"Okay, Ma. Say good night to Scarlett for me. See you tomorrow."

"Call me if you need me, son."

Felix kissed his mother and left the room. He spared a few minutes to check on Casey. She was curled up on her side, her face relaxed and so vulnerable it broke his heart. Unable to resist, he brushed his fingers over her cheek, saw once again the shadows under her eyes.

She curled toward his hand, making him smile, his heart do a tiny somersault. He considered crawling into the bed with her, attempting to kiss her awake. No. He forced himself to walk away because as much as he'd love to run his hands over her breasts and slip inside her body, she needed her rest.

Laughter woke her. Casey went into military mode and used her senses. She was at the resort in Felix's private rooms.

So, who was the female part of the laughter out in the other room?

Jealousy sprang to the fore, taking her by surprise. She didn't have the right. Casey twisted her head to survey the other pillow, satisfied when there was a distinct dent. Felix had slept beside her throughout the night.

More laughter sounded.

"You're awake," Felix said. "Would you like some breakfast? We have coffee. Do you drink that?"

"Yes." Casey hesitated and glanced past Felix to see a woman.

"Good," she said. "You're up. I was starting to wonder if you were ever going to rouse."

Felix put his arm around the woman. "This is my sister Scarlett. Scarlett, this is Casey Seonaid. Scarlett organized your bags to be delivered to my rooms. All your clothes and possessions are here."

"But what about Eva? It was my idea to bring her here for a treat. She'll be worried about me."

"Eva Henry?" Scarlett asked.

"Yes."

"She's with my brother Saber, exploring the other side of the island. He said they'll be several days and won't have com access."

Disappointment seared through Casey, and her shoulders slumped. Her chest tightened, and she had to force herself to breathe through the pinch of pressure. "I'm glad she's enjoying herself. She needed to focus on her business, but I sort of shanghaied her into coming on this trip."

Because she'd been too much of a coward to admit the truth to Eva. That she'd never see her again.

A knock sounded on the door, and it burst open.

"We have a problem," Joe said.

His twin stood right behind him, a grim expression on his handsome face.

"Do you need me?" Scarlett asked.

"Someone cut a hole in the fence again," Joe said.

Casey's gaze cut to Felix. His eyes had gone hard. "Any zylon get through?"

"None that I scented," Sly said. "One of the other guys is watching the hole."

"Right." Felix turned to her and drew her close, then, right in front of his brothers and sister, he kissed her. The exchange wasn't as long or as heated as usual, but when he lifted his head, she was still breathing faster. "Scarlett has a project she wants your help with. I'll try not to be too long."

She acknowledged his words with a nod, but all she could think was he'd kissed her in front of his family. He'd offered his affection without coercion, without concern, without shame. Her fingers rose to her tingling lips and she touched them as Felix followed his brothers out the door.

He'd kissed her openly.

Scarlett chuckled. "You have it bad for my brother. You should see your expression. You look stunned."

Casey felt heat creep into her cheeks.

"Don't act all embarrassed. I think it's cute. Felix is my favorite brother. Do you want something to eat? Ma suggested I take you to her rooms, and we'll eat together while we explain our idea to you. Ma's idea, really," she added. "What are you going to wear today? You have some gorgeous clothes."

Scarlett's cheerful chatter pelted her, another layer to add to her shock. The Mitchell family was nothing like hers, and it made her start to wonder. Why did a person have to live their life in such isolation? Just because the general shouted louder than her, louder than her brothers, louder than her mother, did that mean he was always right?

His order for her to undergo gender change—he'd made it sound logical, sensible. The only decision possible. He'd made it seem *right*.

"Put on this one," Scarlett said, pulling a dress in shades of gold and bronze and silver off a hanger. "Where did you purchase it? I haven't seen anything like this in Dalcon. I'm obviously shopping at the wrong shops. Sanitizer unit is through there."

Casey forced something resembling a smile and fled into the privacy of the unit. While she waited for the cycle to complete, her mind jingled with random thoughts.

The Mitchells were friendly, affectionate, and wanted to spend time with her.

Apart from Eva, no one had ever attempted to seek out her company. There were too many difficulties because of rank, because of her position, because of the general.

The cycle finished, and she returned to the main bedroom, realizing she'd forgotten to gather her underwear.

"Wow, you have a gorgeous figure," Scarlett said.

Casey froze, aware of her nakedness and her body in a way that wasn't familiar. She hurriedly held her dress in front of her.

"Sorry. There I go embarrassing you again. You're so slim, while I have these stupid curves."

Another argument given by the general. She lacked the strength of a man and would never bulk up or be a top soldier because she was physically weak. The change would muscle her up, give her the necessary might.

"Thank you."

Scarlett grinned. "You need to show me where you shop. When I heard you were military, I worried a little. I didn't think you'd make a good match for Felix, but now I see you're perfect." She must have caught something in Casey's expression because her grin widened. "Don't mind me. My brothers tell me I talk too much. They say if I left my computers and technology alone more often and found real people to talk to, I wouldn't feel the need to run off my mouth. I say *pooh* to them."

Affection—pure and simple—colored the complaint.

"Hurry up and get dressed. I'm starving, and I can smell Ma's cinnamon buns. They're my favorite, even though they go straight to my ass and hips. Luckily, I have a fast metabolism."

Casey donned her underwear, a pair of skimpy panties, and a matching bra her aunt had purchased for her as a gift. She sniffed and couldn't smell a thing. "I can't smell anything."

"No, you wouldn't. My brothers and I have exceptional scent detection." Scarlett grinned—wide and bright. "It's a family trait."

Casey slid the dress over her head and pulled the stretchy material into place. It hugged her body and made her feel ultra-feminine—the reason she'd chosen the fabric and made this particular design.

"Gorgeous," Scarlett said. "Shoes?"

Casey found a comfortable pair of shoes and set the design button on the side to the color gold. As she slipped her feet into the shoes, they turned a shade that complemented her dress.

Scarlett's eyes widened. "Get out of town!"

"Pardon?"

"Your shoes. Where did you get them? Do they turn any color you want? Are they expensive? I want some."

"My aunt designs them, and I can change them to any color within their chosen color palette," Casey said. "She has a shop on Dalcon."

"I'll start saving," Scarlett muttered, almost to herself. "Let's go. Ma has put the coffee on."

Casey followed Scarlett from Felix's suite out into the bright solar shine.

"Ah, good timing," Anna Mitchell said as they entered her suite. "I've just pulled the cinnamon buns from the hot cube."

"I know," Scarlett said. "Ma, you have to check out Casey's shoes. Her aunt designed them. They have this little button. Show Ma, Casey. Change them."

"Don't order her around, Scarlett," Anna said. "Good morning, dear. Did you sleep well? You're looking more rested. What a beautiful dress. It suits your coloring to perfection."

"You never told me where you purchased it," Scarlett said.

"I made it," Casey said, the bombardment of conversation almost too much for her to handle. Eva wasn't like this.

Anna and Scarlett stared at her, exchanged a look, then studied her again.

"You made it?" Scarlett asked. "What about your other clothes?"

"I made them too. Mostly, I wear my uniform, so I don't get to wear them very often."

"Oh my god, Ma. She made them, *and* her aunt designed the shoes. Show her, Casey. Will they go bronze or silver?"

Casey changed the dial, and her shoes shifted to bronze and silver stripes.

Scarlett clapped her hands together. "How much are they?"

"Does your aunt live on Dalcon, dear?"

Casey nodded and took a seat at a table when Anna gestured for her to do so.

"Has she ever considered moving?" Anna asked while busying herself with pouring cups of coffee.

"She says she stays on Dalcon because that's where I'm based." A tight sensation wrapped around her chest, making Casey focus on breathing and strain for air.

Scarlett and Anna exchanged glances and seemed to silently communicate because Anna gave a brief nod.

"That's nice, dear," Anna said. "Have one of my cinnamon buns while they're hot."

"Before Felix and the twins arrive. They'll be able to smell them," Scarlett said and slid one on her plate.

"Scarlett and I are considering opening a boutique here at the resort—a new service for our guests. We thought we'd sell clothes, shoes, and perhaps jewelry. What do you think?"

They were asking *her*? Why?

Both women waited patiently, and the silence lengthened. Casey bit into her cinnamon bun to cover her confusion.

"I don't suppose we could talk your aunt into visiting?" Anna asked finally. "We could send her a com right now and invite her. Have you seen her recently?"

Casey shook her head. She seemed to be doing a lot of that with the Mitchells. She swallowed the cinnamon bun. It was delicious. Light and buttery and tasting of fragrant spices. "No, I haven't seen her in person since my last leave."

"That's settled then. We'll invite her for a visit and see if we can entice her to set up a shop here at the resort." She whipped out her com-circle. "What is her frequency, dear?"

Casey told her, bemused by the woman's take-charge manner. In her own way, she'd make a good match for the general, except Casey got the sense that if she objected, the woman would back off.

The door burst open, and Felix and the twins spilled inside. They were followed by another man—the pretty one she'd seen the day before—who appeared enough like the others to make Casey suspect this was another sibling.

The men grabbed cups and plates and joined them around the table. Felix slid in beside her and gave her a quick kiss that sent warmth flooding through her and brought more wonder. This family was like nothing she'd ever experienced before. The brother she hadn't met started a heated discussion with one of the twins—she thought it was Joe. Anna had one ear covered and had her com-circle pressed to the other. She was busy talking.

Scarlett was in a hushed conversation with the other twin. The situation should have brought discomfort and embarrassment at witnessing such intimate and unruly behavior. The general liked to enjoy his meals in silence. Not that her proper mother would ever make loud conversation—not like the Mitchells.

"Is it always like this?"

"Sometimes worse," Felix said. "My oldest brother isn't here, and sometimes our cousins or friends drop around to visit. You look beautiful." He skimmed his fingers over her collarbone, and she felt his touch clear to her toes. Places in between began to hum.

"She's coming," Anna said. "Leo, will you take the shuttle to Dalcon to pick up Elsa Torrens? Casey's aunt."

"Is that a good idea, Ma?" Leo asked with a swift glance at Felix. "And you couldn't have decided this yesterday, so I didn't need to make another trip?"

"It's a brilliant idea," Anna said, unperturbed by her son's disapproval. "Family is important."

"It's the roots that hold us together," the siblings chanted as one.

"It's good to know you listen to me when I'm working on our genealogy," she said serenely, and smiled in Casey's direction. "We have some old family diaries written by an ancestor centuries ago. They're fascinating."

"So fascinating, she named us after our long-ago ancestors," Felix told Casey.

A pang of longing struck at the heart of Casey. They were lucky to have each other, to have the knowledge of their past, and be able to take comfort from their ancestors. So blessed. They had no idea. Maybe that was why she and Eva got on so well together. They understood loneliness.

"Now, Casey. I don't suppose you have a sketchbook of your designs here? If your dress is any indication of your talent, then we want to sell your designs at our store," Anna said in her managing way.

"I saw a sketchpad when I moved your stuff. Can I go and get it?" Scarlett piped up.

Casey shivered, and Felix looked at her in concern.

"Ma, Casey needs to rest."

"No. I mean, yes. It's okay to get my sketchpad."

Scarlett leaped to her feet and disappeared before anyone said another word. She sure moved fast.

"Your parents must be very proud of you," Anna said. "I'm surprised you went into the military when you have such an obvious aptitude for design. Have another cinnamon bun, dear. If you don't take one now, my boys will demolish them all before you get a chance."

Casey stared at her, was aware she'd stiffened and that Felix was frowning at her in concern. But her mind wouldn't go past Anna's words.

Her parents must be proud of her. Military instead of design.

Only Aunt Elsa had ever suggested she follow her talent—her heart—instead of doing what was expected of her by the general.

"One more solar day before I'm scheduled to return to duty," she said to Felix.

"Stay longer," Scarlett urged, returning to the table. "I can sew a little. Design something for me."

More of that warmth whooshed through Casey, heating her body and spirit.

"Me, me, me," one of the twins scolded. "That's all you ever think about."

"Not true," Scarlett retorted. "I've spent the last few months researching—" She broke off with a quick glance at Casey. "Never mind," she said hurriedly. "My point is, it's about time you guys let me do something for myself."

"Scarlett is right," Anna said. "I think it will help."

The conversation confused Casey, and she gave up listening to apply herself to eating her second cinnamon bun. Delicious. She licked her fingers to make sure she got all the sugar and spices sticking to them.

"Keep that up, and I'm dragging you to my suite and tying you to my bed."

Casey froze, felt her eyes widen and heat steal into her face. She grabbed her coffee and took a sip of the strong beverage. Maybe the liquid would supply the jolt she required to restore her balance.

Felix chuckled, and his siblings grinned and fell quiet, making her and Felix the center of attention.

"Casey and I are going for a walk," he announced. "We'll be checking the perimeter if anyone needs us."

"Your aunt will arrive later this afternoon. I'll send for you when she arrives. We'll have afternoon tea here in my suite, just us girls. Son, you must—"

"I know, Ma," Felix said. "Don't worry. I have everything under control."

Felix hustled her out the door, his arm slung around her shoulders. She'd noticed he liked to touch her, and she'd come to enjoy his casual affection. If she ever—

No. There would be no family for her, no children because the transformation would leave her sterile. Most gender-changers couldn't sire offspring, and she'd end up the same way. Some of the happiness that had bloomed in her since waking seeped away.

"I thought we'd walk the perimeter and double-check the compound fences," Felix said, guiding her to the right and along a gravel path. Crimson flowers covered pale-blue bushes, the flowers cheerful and bright. When they turned, green and gold plants with apricot-colored flowers bordered the path. In the distance, she heard the rush of the waves and caught the briny scent of the jade sea.

"And the other reason I suggested you come with me..." He swirled her around a corner and into the shadows cast by a copse of tall trees. "I wanted to kiss you good morning. A proper kiss."

He suited actions to words, pressing her against the rough amber bark of a tree trunk and trapping her there. His mouth hit hers, crushing them together with heat and urgency. He made a rough sound deep in his chest and stroked his tongue across the seam of her lips. She opened to him, and he immediately took advantage, the kiss becoming ravenous. Determined.

And she loved every moment.

She gripped his shoulders and hung on, participating in the dueling of tongues, stoking the passion between them.

"Fuck," he muttered when he lifted his head. His eyes gleamed, the pupils glowing in a strange manner. They...

They had elongated.

"I have to take you." He slid his hand down her hip and stole under the short skirt of her dress. "Panties?"

The surprise in his voice brought a choked laugh. "I couldn't visit your mother and not wear panties. That's all kinds of wrong. Scarlett would have known, for one."

"We'll take care of that." He grasped one side of them, gave a jerk, and her panties came away in his hand. "I'll buy you more—if I must."

"Please," she said, not sure what else to say since everything with Felix seemed out of her normal realm.

As he spoke, he worked the opening of his trews and pulled out his cock. His hand went between her legs. "You're not wet enough, sweetheart. Not for what I have in mind."

Before she could comment, he sank to his knees in front of her. He gripped her hips, silently encouraged her to widen her stance, and gave her a firm lick. A sensual jolt struck, along with amazement at the rasp of his tongue. Talented tongue, she thought, half dazed at the suddenness of the event. Felix wanted her enough that he'd risk others seeing them, catching them unawares. Her stomach roiled, but it was in a good way, with excitement and acute anticipation as he licked and sucked her flesh.

An ache sprang up in her pussy, and a tremor swept the length of her body. She grasped his shoulders for balance because her legs seemed to lose their strength and wobbled in a non-military manner.

He lifted his mouth away from her heated flesh, and she let out a groan of disappointment. He laughed, the sound pleased and joyful, and grinned up at her in a rakish way that trapped her breath in her lungs. Her juices shone around his mouth, and as she watched, he licked his lips, his wicked smile widening.

"You taste delicious."

He stood and closed the distance between them, backing her against the tree trunk again. His steely cock told her where his mind was headed, and she liked the direction of his thoughts. Memories to hoard, at least until—

No, she refused to think of the future.

The present—that was where she should dwell.

A sharp tap on her chin jerked her securely to the now.

"Where do you go? I've noticed before. You zone out. You don't have to suffer my touch," Felix snapped. "Not if I bother you so much you need to send your mind elsewhere."

"No." She couldn't let him think such a thing. "No, it's not that. I have...a problem," she said in a rush. "My mind keeps circling it, no matter how much I wish it away."

"Tell me."

"I can't." She closed her eyes, her heart singed by the caring in his expression. "I—I can't."

"Okay, sweetheart." He brushed his fingers across her cheek. "I'll just have to fuck you so good and hard your mind turns to mush, and then we'll walk around the compound and work on tiring you out until you're exhausted, so you'll sleep tonight."

"I'm departing soon."

His hands tensed on her body. "I don't want you to leave."

"I have to report for...d-duty. It's my job."

"But you don't like your job. It makes you unhappy."

Casey felt her mouth drop open. How...she'd never said anything, done anything to indicate otherwise. Most people didn't see through her perfect military posture and behavior to the woman beneath. "It's my duty."

"We'll see," he said and kissed her hard, demanding a response from her. His hands crawled beneath her dress to cup her bare bottom. Then he was lifting her, filling her with his hardness, curling her legs around his hips, and pressing her against the tree.

She clung to him, let him do all the work because he did it so well. He made her soar, the pleasure growing from a spark and swelling with each decisive thrust of his cock. The pulse at her throat beat a wild tattoo and her heart raced as he bent to increase his assault on her senses with a hot and demanding kiss.

Sensations spiraled down, took flight, and then she was soaring, internal muscles clamping around his cock. She gasped and cried out while clinging to his masculine contours. He groaned against her mouth, pistoned his hips to shove deep and stopped moving, the hard ridge of his cock filling her.

Pleasure was still coursing through her body when he lifted her off him and set her on her feet. He crushed her to his body in a fierce hug.

"That's a much better way to start the day." He rearranged himself and refastened his trousers.

She stood there, chest rising and falling rapidly, still quivering internally. Wow. Incredible. She was never aware of her body in this way. Her flesh tingled and her breasts throbbed with heaviness while her backside still ached from the spanking the other day.

"Hey," he said in a quiet voice. He tugged down her dress and smoothed the bodice back in place. "Turn around. You'll have bits of bark clinging to your dress."

She turned as instructed and shivered again when he ran his hand down her back and over her buttocks.

"We'll stop by the restrooms so you can do a quick cleanup."

She gave a startled nod, not used to men referring to feminine issues. Another reason the general had put forward as an argument for his plan. Male equals no messy problems. A win-win situation for all concerned.

Felix took her hand and threaded their fingers together before leading her toward the beach and the restroom and changing sheds.

An employee was raking up leaves, and another was planting a new garden. Casey tried to tug her hand free, but Felix refused to allow it and stopped to chat with the employees. He slung his arm around her shoulders in casual ownership while he discussed a couple of tasks he required them to complete during the coming days.

Once that was done, he continued to the restrooms.

"I'll wait outside for you. Don't take long because it's important to recheck the fences."

His smile of approval when she returned a short time later was blinding. He gave her a kiss, nuzzled her neck, gave her a quick lick at the spot where shoulder and neck met then reclaimed her hand. At least she'd stopped jumping when he reached for her. The constant physical contact was relaxing and kind of nice.

She let him lead her away from the main resort area to a narrow path that followed the compound fence. It was a tall barrier, higher than her head, and she was taller than average. A fine mesh covered the bottom part and reached as high as her waist.

Felix walked ahead of her now, his focus on the fence. "Hell, there's another bloody hole. I checked this sector before I came to collect you."

"Someone is cutting the fence on purpose? Why?"

"Because someone wants the resort to fail," Felix said in disgust.

"Any idea who it is?"

"Not a one. We're doing irregular checks, have organized a team to monitor the boundaries, but we haven't discovered anything suspicious."

"An inside job?" Casey felt a prickle at her back, as if someone were spying on them. She turned slowly and casually surveyed the area outside the compound. Maybe it was imagination, yet...

No. A green man was standing in a copse of trees outside the resort. His clothing was a bit weird since he wore a pink cloth to cover his masculine equipment, and that was all.

Casey moved closer to Felix and whispered. "A man is hiding in the trees outside the fence. You'll have to look carefully because he blends well with the pink and green foliage."

Felix shifted his body and scanned the area she'd indicated. "Can't see anything." His nostrils flared when he sniffed the air. "I can smell something, though. It's almost a gamey scent."

"He didn't look like one of your employees."

"We'd better get supplies to fix the hole," Felix said. "I should've brought something with me, but I didn't think I'd need to fix a hole again so soon."

"It's a pretty spot. You want me to stay here to guard the breach?"

"Sure, enjoy the sun, but don't get tempted to go exploring. Okay? I don't like the idea of strangers around the resort."

"I'm a soldier. I know how to defend myself."

Felix frowned but paused to give her one of his lazy, toe-curling kisses. Talk about racking up memories. The thought drove away the pleasure of the moment, and she was glad when he strode off to retrieve tools. She didn't want him to witness the pain in her, the way her lips and chin started to tremble despite her attempt to hold them in a firm line.

She sat on the soft grass, crossed her arms, and rocked herself while focusing on the spot where she'd sighted the man.

A sharp chirp to her right, a scuffle in the long pink grasses, ripped her gaze off the fixed point. She scanned the ornamental grasses and caught the glitter of a big brown eye. A delicate paw poked out from the plants, followed by a nose—not pointed but quite flat.

The muscles of Casey's stomach tightened, but she remained still. Was it one of those zylon creatures? Eva had seen one. She'd attempted to pet it but a huge black cat had grabbed and killed the creature seconds before Eva could stroke the zylon's soft-looking fur. She'd read the warning signs inside their bungalow and seen the picture of the creature, but they looked so cute.

"Aw, you've got babies." Every instinct urged her to pet one and coo over it, which proved how off-balance she'd become. Maybe she had a budding death wish?

Death by a fluffy creature or personality wipe by nanotechnology?

Decisions. Decisions.

"Casey, don't make any sudden moves. It makes them pounce." Felix's calm voice came from behind her. She kept her gaze fixed on the creatures and waited. Apparently, the gods didn't want her to die today.

Without warning, a huge black cat pounced and grabbed the biggest zylon. The creatures let out squawks of alarm and fled for the safety of the grasses. The black cat was quicker though, and it dispatched every zylon before a single one escaped.

Then the cat turned its gaze on *her*.

Casey flinched but didn't bolt as her brain urged her to do. Instead, she stared into the vivid green eyes.

Maybe death was on her agenda for today after all.

CHAPTER SIX

F elix stared at Casey, his heart pulsing so fast he thought it might bound out of his chest. He called up his human form and shifted, leaping at Casey as soon as he could and hauling her to her feet. His hands went up and down her body. He checked her bare legs for signs of blood.

"Did it bite you?"

"No, you—that was *you*." Her mouth worked, but no more sound emerged.

He waited, wary, part of him terrified she'd find his dual nature unpalatable. Some women couldn't deal with the fact their mates became huge hairy beasts on a whim.

"You..." she said again. "You have two forms?"

"I'm a feline shifter, sweetheart." He drew closer, and when she didn't scream, he indulged his need to hold her. Fuck, he'd nearly expired when he saw the zylon with her pups. The creatures were cantankerous at the best of times but became ultra-aggressive if they thought their pups were in danger.

"The rest of your family...?"

"Yes, and a lot of our employees too."

"Your mother?"

"No, not my mother. Her parents were both shifters, but she has never been able to shift for some reason. Our father passed on the gene to us."

"And you'll pass the ability on to your children?"

"*Our* children," Felix said, the idea pleasing him immensely.

"I-I don't think I'll ever have children."

Something in her expression warned him not to push, and she appeared fragile, with shadows in her eyes hinting at her emotional turmoil. Damn. He'd thought after a good night of sleep, she might share her inner demons.

"What's wrong, sweetheart?"

"You're naked. Someone might come along and see."

"It would only be an employee. They're used to seeing me in this state."

She plucked at the hem of her dress, her body tense in his arms. Hell, whatever was wrong, he'd fix it because the more time he spent with her, the more he liked her. He wanted to spend the rest of his life making her happy. Sure, it had only been a few days, but as Ma said, the mind knew what the mind knew. His parents' courtship had been equally rapid, and they'd had many happy years together until a motor vehicle accident had stolen their father.

"Casey, you can tell me anything. Let me help."

"I have to leave tomorrow." Her voice was hoarse, and it wobbled on the edge of tearful.

"Stay."

"I can't. I have to report for duty."

Felix nuzzled her neck, breathing in her familiar scent, the whiff of their earlier lovemaking. There was no way in hell he'd let her leave the resort or his suite tomorrow, and if he had to, he'd tie her to his bed to prevent her departure. She mightn't realize it yet, but they belonged together. They'd deal with the consequences. His family would help.

Time to change the subject and divert her mind from thoughts of separation.

"Did you see the man again?"

"No, just the zylon. You weren't gone for long."

The tension seeped from her muscles as they chatted, and she leaned into his body, a fact that pleased him.

"Why don't you alarm the fence?" she asked. "You could rig a silent alarm and perhaps catch the person responsible for cutting holes. It can't be the man I saw, though, because the way the fence material is cut suggests the opening was made from the inside."

"Which points to one of our employees," Felix said. "Scarlett should be able to come up with an alarm system, and you and I can install it tonight."

"It might take longer than that to design and install—"

"Scarlett is a whiz with technology. There is nothing my sister can't do, and I'm a fair hand with anything mechanical. Between us, we'll sort it. Let's get this fence mended and get back to see Scarlett."

He turned her head and tried to claim a swift kiss.

"You are not kissing me again, Felix," Casey said, her nose wrinkling in distaste. "I saw what you did to those zylon. You need to clean your teeth before you come anywhere near me with that mouth."

Felix grinned, cheered despite missing out on a proper smooch with his lady. Her imperious manner rated several grades above her previous despondency. Things were looking up.

"Casey!"

Without warning, Casey found herself in her aunt's perfumed embrace once more, and it felt like coming home. After a brief introduction to Felix and his family, they were left alone to visit. She blinked back the sting of tears and held on to her aunt's curvy frame.

Elsa was half a head shorter than Casey and dressed in one of the designs they'd worked on together last solar year. She wore a pair of her special shoes to match the delicate blue of her calf-length gown.

"It's so good to see you, child." Elsa pulled back and her happy smile faded. "Are you ill? You don't look good. You've lost weight. You're obviously not sleeping. I thought a few days at the resort with Eva would be good for you."

Casey couldn't meet her aunt's concerned gaze. Shame filled her, her mind too exhausted to spin a credible story. Self-loathing struck at the idea of lying to her beloved aunt, the woman who'd championed her since she was a child, and given Casey every memorable moment in her life, some interests to fill the yawning gaps in her days.

She couldn't do it.

"The general has arranged nanotechnology for me once I report back to duty," she blurted before she could stop herself.

An appalled expression slammed over her aunt's face. "To do what?" she demanded.

"A sex change."

"Low-down slimy *millock* worm!" her aunt snarled. "And you've agreed to this?"

"I wasn't given much choice," Casey said, averting her gaze in shame.

"But it's *your* life! What did he say?"

"He said I couldn't progress any higher in the ranks because I'm female. I'm too weak, both physically and mentally."

"No, not that. What *threats* did he issue?"

"He said if—if I didn't go ahead with the transformation, he'd disown me and make sure I was demoted to the troops. He said I'd lose everything."

"You can come and live with me," her aunt said. "I love you, child. I think of you as my daughter."

"The general knows that. He said if I went to you, he'd destroy your business." He'd also intimated he'd send in black ops to take her aunt out, but Casey couldn't tell her aunt. *Scurvy sky pirates*, she couldn't fathom even the general stooping that low.

"The man is a *millock* maggot," Elsa snapped. "I suspected he had something similar done to your mother. She transformed practically overnight. That was before you were born. He's *not* going to do that to you," she said in a fierce tone. "I suppose he even has a name picked out for you."

"Arthur," Casey said in a faint tone.

"*Gah!* Isn't that one of his middle names?"

Casey nodded, unable to speak past the ache in her throat.

"Have you told that young man of yours what your father intends to do? You're not going to go through with it." Elsa gripped her forearms and squeezed to the point of pain. "Casey, no matter what the general says, you are perfect now. You will not give in to his blackmail. Did you tell your young man?"

"I've only known him a few days."

"Rubbish, that man is halfway in love with you. It won't take much effort on your part to push him the rest of the way. You have feelings for him. Don't deny it. I saw it on your face when you introduced me to him and the rest of his family."

"You can't tell him. Please!"

Elsa scowled. "I don't agree. You should tell him, but very well. I'll keep quiet. For the present," she added, a warning in her tone. "Now...I packed your sewing machine and brought some fabrics plus a dozen pairs of shoes. I also brought your design books. I love the idea of having our designs in the resort. You should think about staying here and helping to set up the store. You could work on more designs and even design to order."

"I can't do that."

"Why not?" her aunt demanded. "You've tried for years to get your father to notice you, to show his love and approval. I tell you, the man is a *millock* maggot and has less personality. Child, you have to accept some men can't or won't show their emotions."

"The general—"

"See, that's an example right there. He won't even let you call him 'father'."

A tap on the door put a halt to further arguments. Casey hated disagreeing with her aunt, but she did have a point. Despite her years of hard work, the general had never shown her a scrap of love or approval. Her older brothers gained his respect, but not her. A part of her wondered, if she went through with the nanotechnology, would his opinion really change?

Experience propelled her to admit the truth. Even as a man, she'd be second best because she hadn't been born that way. She'd be a *made* man.

Scarlett stuck her head in the door. "Ma said that your luggage has arrived and to come to her suite when you're ready. She has afternoon tea, and we need to get there before my brothers descend on the place. They can smell her scones from miles away." Scarlett winked at Casey. "So can I. She's just taken them out of the hot cube."

Casey found herself smiling back at Scarlett. Felix had obviously told her she knew about their dual natures. A big cat. She needed to get him to transform for her again because she'd like to stroke his fur.

"I don't believe I've ever had a scone," Aunt Elsa said. "We're ready, aren't we, Casey?"

"Sure." Their conversation wasn't going anywhere.

"I can't wait to see more of your designs, Casey," Scarlett said. "And your shoes, Elsa! Ma said you were bringing shoes for us to examine. I've been starved of all things fashionable," she complained, leading the way to her mother's suite.

"Can you sew?" Aunt Elsa asked Scarlett.

"A little, but I'd like to learn more. I can't draw to save myself, so I'd need to have some sort of pattern."

Casey trailed her aunt and Scarlett, her mind a mired mess of thoughts. It felt as if a clock was ticking down in her brain, racing faster and faster toward D-day.

Tomorrow. Tomorrow. *Tomorrow.*

"I like your aunt," Felix said later that night.

"You have the seal of approval from her too."

"Good to know." He opened the door to his suite of rooms and ushered her inside. "But I've been counting the minutes until I could get you alone."

Casey forced a smile, and her attempt must have lacked something because he cast her a concerned look.

"I'll get Ma to make you another sleep tonic."

"No, I don't need to sleep tonight." She'd have plenty of time to rest once the nanotechnology process started. They'd put her into an induced coma to allow the technology to work.

Gods, no! She didn't want to do this!

A choked cry escaped her, the internal pain too much to contain.

"What is it, sweetheart?" Felix pulled her against his body and wrapped her in his arms. His care, his interest in her well-being, only made the pain roll up and expand until she feared she would choke. Tears burned her eyes, and she buried her face against his chest with a tortured groan.

She felt herself being lifted and clung to him—her rock.

"Let's get you into bed," he said.

Felix helped her undress and settled her under the covers. A few moments later, he slid into the sleep-bed beside her.

"Lights out," he murmured, and the room darkened.

Casey was grateful when he didn't ask more questions. Instead, he held her and gave her the comfort she'd never received from anyone other than her aunt.

A sharp, piercing sound woke her just as she'd started to drift. She rolled out of bed and was crouched in a defensive position before she'd even processed a thought.

"Lights on," Felix snapped. "It's the alarm on the fence. A simple one until Scarlett can get the silent alarm online." He picked up his com and called his siblings. "Stay here while we take care of this."

"No. Let me get my weapon, and I'll come too. I can help. Let me use my training." She scrambled into comfortable clothing and sat to pull on socks and boots, used to dressing at top speed. "It's got to be one of your employees or someone who lives at the resort. They're hardly likely to be that dangerous."

The crude alarm continued to wail inside his room, and he gave a quick nod, apparently persuaded by her argument. "If you get hurt, I'm gonna paddle your ass," he warned.

"I'm an experienced soldier." She grabbed her weapon from the false bottom of her bag and turned to see Felix in cat form.

He let out a low feline bark. An order since he couldn't open the door with four paws.

Once she opened it, he trotted through and barked again. Probably an order for her to take care. Since she'd already suffered through one spanking, she didn't intend to incur his wrath and gain another punishment. She trotted after him, eyes scanning their surroundings.

A low growl came from their right, and two other cats arrived. Casey stared, fascinated despite the situation. They conversed with grunts, growls, and a different set of barks when two more cats loped over to join them. That done, they split, two cats going in one direction and the other pair heading to the right. Felix nudged her leg and trotted off, clearly expecting her to follow.

Lights from the resort lit most of the way, but the trees and vegetation cast dark shadows and created lots of possible places for someone to hide. Felix stopped and lifted his head. He was scenting, she realized.

Felix moved on and halted several times to test the air. When he stopped by a dark bush, he grunted and set off at a fast pace.

Casey trotted after him. The military had trained her to run silently, but Felix was better than their best.

He slowed, halted, and Casey stopped too, allowing her senses to stretch outward into the night. The silence seemed complete, but there was an odd scent on the air. A musky smell. Felix grunted and slid through the darkness. Casey couldn't creep through the undergrowth with the same ease. Instead, she rounded obstacles, moving cautiously. The scent grew stronger and stronger until she could no longer breathe through her nose with comfort.

Her stomach roiled, and she dry-heaved. Casey bent from the waist and breathed through her mouth. Gods! That smell was enough to turn anyone's stomach.

Casey straightened and kept moving. The musky scent grew even worse, if that was possible, and she had no idea where Felix was now since she couldn't make him out in the darkness. Black cat. Night. It was a bad combination.

Casey made it to the fence and used the barrier as a guide. That smell—whatever it was—was disgusting. She hadn't noticed anything like it around the resort.

Eventually her hand met air. She'd found the breach in the perimeter.

Gods! She made a low gagging sound; even breathing through her mouth wasn't helping her get past the stench.

Footsteps. *Scurvy sky pirates!* Someone was nearby, and she instinctively knew they were the source of the puke-wrenching stink.

Rough hands seized her as she gagged again, this time losing her dinner.

She was hustled through the hole in the fence. A familiar gruff bark, answered by another, told her Felix and his brothers were near.

"Felix!" she screamed. "The hole in the fence is here!"

She played dead, sagging in her captor's arms.

Surprised by her move, her abductor staggered and almost dropped her. Casey surged into motion and darted away, but her snatcher was quick. He grabbed her again.

"Stop fighting," he growled. "I don't want to hurt you." His accent was broad, difficult to make out the words. "Stop," he said, his tone sharp and determined.

Casey stilled and got her first good look at one of the captors. They were tall and lean, their only clothing the pink loincloth. Their hair was long and matted into lots of different strands. Their green faces and features were almost humanoid—golden-brown round eyes, broad noses, and large lips. Their skin was a mottled green with faint gold swirls, and it felt sticky. Their teeth were a strong and startling white contrast to their drab green faces.

Then there was the smell—pungent and gamey—and it seemed to come off their skin. When she took a closer look, she noticed it seemed to be a type of grease or fat, and they'd plastered it over their entire bodies. Not so good for a surprise attack. The enemy would smell them from miles away.

"What do you want?" she demanded, aware the warrior was checking her out with the same intense scrutiny.

"That is for my chief to divulge."

Casey sucked in a breath, prepared to scream, and the stench hit her again. "What is that god-awful stink?"

Her captor chuckled. "A good defense mechanism, eh? You get used to it after a while."

A bird call sounded, and her captor straightened, his fingers a band around her upper arm. "We leave now."

"No. *No*. My man will be looking for me. Leave me here, and no one will get hurt." Stupid creature. He hadn't even searched her for weapons. She had her laser-blaster tucked in the small of her back.

"That is good." Her abductor sounded unperturbed. He propelled her along a narrow track into the trees. Now that she was away from the resort lights, her eyesight adjusted. There were five other men aside from her captor, and their collective stink was enough to make her eyes water. At least Felix would manage to track easily if she didn't manage to free herself.

Thoughts of Felix made a faint smile curl her lips. He wasn't going to be happy, and her backside tingled at the idea of another spanking.

Fuck! They had Casey.

Felix let out a gruff bark and shifted while he waited for his siblings to join him beside the hole in the fence.

Almost immediately, they slid through the jungle and stopped beside him, shifting also when they saw he wanted to talk.

"This hole was made from the outside," he said. "We have intruders this time rather than someone within the resort."

"What is that stench?" Scarlett demanded. "It makes my nose twitch."

"That's the trail," Felix said drily. "Did anyone see them?"

"Yeah. They looked like tribesman," Joe said. "Wore loincloths."

"I thought they looked like two-legged frogs," Scarlett said.

Sly sniggered, and Scarlett elbowed him.

"Cut it out," Felix snapped. "Casey said she saw someone when we were checking the fence earlier today. I didn't see them."

"You would have smelled them," Scarlett said.

Felix shook his head. "Not this afternoon."

"What do you want to do?" Leo asked.

"Follow them and get my mate back," Felix said. "Now that I've found her, there's no way in hell I intend to lose her. Scarlett, you stay."

"No way. I can defend myself."

"That's what Casey said," Felix muttered. "She's gonna have a sore backside when I retrieve her."

"Huh," Scarlett said. "And Ma wonders why I don't show any interest in males. You're all bossy. Why should I give up my freedom?"

"I can think of a suitable punishment for you too," Felix promised.

"I'm not going home," Scarlett snapped.

"Fine. Let's go," Felix said. "I don't want Casey with them for any longer than necessary."

The siblings shifted and slipped through the fence, silently following the trail.

After ten minutes of fast tracking, Felix slowed when he heard voices.

"I can't go any faster," Casey said in a tone he hadn't heard from her before. "I've hurt my foot."

"I carry you."

"I'm not getting closer to that stink."

Felix smirked.

A sharp scream sounded. Casey's scream—and Felix snarled in fury.

"I told you my man will come!" Casey said, her voice pitched loud.

Clever girl.

"No. No! Carrying me upside down will make me sick."

Felix gave a gruff bark, and he and his siblings burst through the forest to surround the men.

The men in loincloths—*pink* loincloths—bunched and kept Casey in the middle of their group.

Felix gave another gruff bark and shifted. "You all right, Casey?"

"I'm fine."

Felix watched her elbow her way through the men. They didn't object. Instead, they jabbered excitedly amongst themselves. Felix didn't understand a word.

"Or I will be when I can breathe again."

Felix couldn't blame her for that. Their collective stench was making his eyes water.

"What?" she demanded, turning back to the men. "*Scurvy sky pirates!*"

One of the men jabbered at her, and Casey jabbered back.

"What's going on?" Felix asked.

"They have more warriors back at their camp and intend to attack the resort unless they get a black cat."

"But we're *shifters*," Felix said.

"They didn't realize that." Casey jabbered some more and groaned. "They have a chief, and the chief has a daughter who heard about the black cats. She wants one for her age-anniversary gift. You'd better show them the others are shifters. They're not convinced."

"Shift," Felix ordered, and his siblings transformed, which set the natives jabbering again.

"Why can't we understand them? We all have the universal implants," Scarlett said.

"My military implant has more languages," Casey replied.

Felix curled his hands into fists. "How many warriors?"

"Two score," Casey said after another quick conversation.

"What are we going to do?" Joe asked.

Felix frowned and tried to think what Saber would do. No way in hell could they withstand an attack of two hundred warriors. They had their guests to think about, as well as their employees.

"Would they consider a smaller cat?" he asked Casey. "In a different color?"

"Jacey's cat has a litter," Scarlett said. "Good idea, bro."

Casey asked the warriors, and Felix waited anxiously for their reply. It was the only solution he could think of because he sure as hell wasn't sending any of the shifters to act as a pet for the chief's daughter.

"They'll ask the chief," Casey said. "But they're saying I must go with them to explain and to serve as hostage."

"No!" Felix exploded.

"Felix, that might be the only solution."

He looked at the tribesmen. "If she stays with you, I want one of your warriors with us."

Casey gave an approving nod, but it didn't ease Felix in the slightest. She translated for the warriors, and they held a heated discussion.

"What's going on?" Felix demanded. They were getting upgrades to their implants. He'd get Scarlett on the job as soon as Casey was safely back at the resort.

The jabbering stopped, and Casey turned to him. "They refuse to release me until they talk to their chief, but they understand you're upset at them for taking your woman." Her nose wrinkled. "They'll send their most influential warrior with you to see the cat so that he may report back to the chief as to the suitability of the gift."

"Where are they from?" Felix demanded.

She asked, and the color fled her cheeks. "A two-day march from here."

Damn, she was still intending to leave. As long as her safety was guaranteed, maybe this would aid his cause. "Fine. Tell the warrior who's coming with us that if he makes the slightest wrong move, we will kill him. We will show him the cats and he will choose the one he thinks is most suitable for the chief's daughter. Is this agreeable?"

More jabbering ensued while Felix signaled his siblings to come closer.

"What do you think?" he murmured in a low voice, just in case they understood them.

"We don't have any option," Sly said. "If they have that many warriors, we're in trouble. We need to be at peace with them."

Felix nodded. His thinking exactly.

Scarlett squeezed his arm. "Don't worry. Casey is handling herself well. She's not a nincompoop like Lori. She's keeping her head, showing her military training."

Felix nodded, agreeing with his sister's assessment but not liking it any better. He didn't want to leave her alone with the natives. There was no telling what they might do.

"They've agreed with your suggestion, Felix." She closed the distance between them, speaking sharply when one of the warriors attempted to stop her. She pressed her palm against his chest, right over his heart. "I truly don't think they'll hurt me."

"Yet they had to sneak into the resort. They didn't think of approaching us in a civilized manner."

"I'll suggest it to them should they need to contact you again." Casey smiled at him, and he saw it was only a little forced. "This is what I trained to do, at least part of it is. I'll be fine."

Before he could offer an argument or give instructions, she kissed him. Despite their audience, she made the kiss slow, tender, and emotion-filled.

Felix gripped her shoulders, pulled her flush with his body, and kissed her back.

"Bro," Scarlett said. "It's time to go."

Felix's hands opened then closed on Casey's shoulders again. "Anything happens to you, and it's war. You tell them I'll be coming after the chief and then his daughter. You tell them I won't stop until I have you back."

CHAPTER SEVEN

C asey tramped after the warriors in front of her, their path taking them through the jungle. Late afternoon, and the air was close. Luckily, she'd long ago stopped smelling the stench that came with the warriors. Her shirt stuck to her chest, and she craved a cool dip in the ocean.

The heat didn't seem to bother the warriors in their loincloths. Nor did the scarlet biting insects that dive-bombed her arms every few minutes.

The warrior who'd taken over the leadership after the head one went with Felix, called a halt and barked out a series of orders. Casey didn't bother listening too closely. Instead, she sank onto a fallen log and tugged her shirt away from her clammy torso.

One of the warriors handed her a flask. Water, he explained, and after a suspicious sniff, she took several swallows. She handed it back and slapped at an insect.

"The stench repels them," the warrior said, showing a flash of white teeth.

"So you wear that grease stuff all the time?"

"Comes through skin." He gestured at his green-and-gold-swirled chest. "Keeps bugs away and body cool. Wash off when swim in river."

"Glory be." She had visions of the men making love with their women, the females wearing pegs on their noses. Heck, for all she knew, the worse the scent, the greater the attraction. Some tribes had peculiar customs.

Two of the warriors returned with fruit and they handed some to her. She watched the others bite into the bright-pink flesh and decided it was safe for her to do the same. After walking all day, her stomach was protesting the lack of fuel.

Then they were off again. Casey fell into line and resumed walking and eating her fruit. It was only when darkness started to fall, and they'd exited the jungle and come to a stop by a river, that the leader signaled it was time to camp for the night.

She should have already been back on Dalcon. Tomorrow, she was supposed to catch a shuttle, report to the army base, and then catch another to the medical center—a secret one on the other side of the planet.

That wasn't going to happen.

Instead the decision had been taken out of her hands.

Casey recognized a feeling of excitement—and realized she didn't care about the stigma of going AWOL.

She no longer wished to chase the general's approval. Spending time with Felix, with his family, had shown her a choice, how her life could be if she was brave enough to take the steps to make it happen.

Anna Mitchell had offered her a job at the resort. She could help start the boutique, and once it was up and running, she could focus on designing. Anna had also offered Aunt Elsa an outlet for her shoes with a commission.

Casey helped collect the leafy plants the warrior showed her and followed suit when they turned them into beds. Dinner was more fruit and water—more than she'd had on a lot of past missions. They took turns swimming in the river and allowed Casey to bathe too. The warriors swam well and she discovered—when they removed their footwear, their feet were webbed—allowing them to swim with great speed.

The warriors settled down for the night and refreshed, Casey lay on her leafy bed. Aunt Elsa had hinted if Casey settled on Tiraq, then she'd relocate and run her business from the resort. She wanted to be close to Casey. Proof her aunt loved her unconditionally.

The sting at the back of her eyes didn't take her by surprise this time. Felix wanted her to stay with him, and Aunt Elsa approved. She'd liked all the members of the Mitchell family. In truth, it was difficult not to enjoy the rambunctious bunch.

For the first time since her last meeting with the general, she fell asleep with something other than fear. She fell asleep with hope in her heart.

Felix's gut twisted as he showed the warrior through the resort to the employee accommodations. Now fully clothed, he indicated the warrior should wait and knocked on a door.

Jacey Patel opened the door, her smile widening when she spotted Felix. Her nose wrinkled next, and she let out a sneeze. "Pardon me. Ma, Felix is here to visit."

"Jacey, it's *you* I've come to visit. Are you still looking for homes for your kittens?"

"Yes. I have two left."

"Could we see them?" Felix asked.

"We?" Jacey sneezed again.

Felix gestured the warrior forward. "Maybe we could come around the back to the garden?"

"The kittens are out there with their mother," Jacey said.

Felix led the warrior around the back and waited for Jacey. Her mother appeared beside her and sent a querying glance at Felix.

"My friend here lives on the island. His chief is looking for a birthday gift for his daughter, and they're interested in a kitten."

"For a pet or for food?" Jacey asked.

"A pet," Felix said, hoping he was telling the truth. "Can we see them?"

"Jacey, show them the kittens," her mother said.

The teenager called, and the kittens, plus their mother, came running.

The warrior gasped and said something in his quick jabber.

Felix crouched and clicked his finger. One cat, a curious ginger, trotted over, and Felix picked it up. He ran his hand over the kitten's body, and it started purring.

The warrior made a soft sound, not far from a chuckle, and Felix handed the kitten to him. The warrior held it carefully and copied the stroking motion Felix had used. Thankfully, the stench didn't bother the kitten, and it licked the warrior on the arm.

The other kitten, both brave and curious, rubbed against the warrior's legs and gave a plaintive meow. The warrior chuckled again and stooped to scoop up the other kitten.

Enough of the polite stuff.

"Which one?" Felix asked, pointing to the ginger cat then its black-and-white friend.

The warrior seemed to understand. He looked at both and nodded, turning away and leaving with the pair.

Okay, both it was. He could deal with that.

"Jacey, do you have a cage we can borrow? And food for two

days?" Felix asked before running after the warrior. He held up his hand in a stop signal before miming eating and pointing to the kittens. Thank goodness, the man seemed to understand.

Felix touched his arm and indicated they should return to Jacey.

With the kittens in a carry cage, food for several days plus some food for himself, Felix and the warrior were leaving for the village when Elsa found him.

"Has Casey left?" Elsa demanded. "I was sure she'd stay rather than go through with that damn fool idea of the general's."

"No, she hasn't gone," Felix said. "She's still on the island, and I'm going to meet her."

Elsa clutched his arm in an almost-painful grip. "Please don't let her leave. Promise me you won't."

Felix frowned, desperate to ask what she was talking about, but aware of the warrior's impatience, he quickly told Elsa the blunt truth. "I have no intention of letting her leave the island. She stays with me."

Elsa let out a hard breath. "Good. That's good."

"Casey and I will be back soon," Felix promised. "A couple of days. I have my com-circle. The family can contact us if necessary."

Felix and the warrior—Gus, he'd discovered after listening to the man speak and point to his chest—traveled quickly despite having the kittens as an encumbrance.

The sooner he got to Casey, the happier he'd feel.

Two days later, Military Medical Headquarters, Dalcon

"General Seonaid on the com, Doctor."

Dr. Phillips winced, searched his office for some means of escape, an excuse to avoid speaking with the man, and failed. "Very well, Soosan. Put him through. Ah, General. How are you today?

What can I do for you?"

"How is the nanotechnology progressing with Captain Seonaid?" the general demanded. On the monitor, a large man leaned back in his chair and tapped his fingers on his desk, the very image of an impatient man who thought everyone should jump at his orders.

"Captain Seonaid didn't arrive for her initial assessment. I assumed she'd had second thoughts about the process. After all, they're very radical changes, and final once they're done."

The general straightened in his seat and leaned forward. "Didn't turn up for her appointment?"

"No." And he could hardly blame her. This case was most irregular. Her file contained no psychiatric evaluation, and he'd had no patient meeting to explain the procedure and the possible consequences. Instead, he'd been ordered to prepare a brochure for the captain to peruse at her leisure while she was on vacation.

"Why wasn't I informed?" the general demanded.

"As I said, I assumed Captain Seonaid had second thoughts. It's not unusual."

"I ordered Captain Seonaid to report to you as soon as she returned from her vacation," the general thundered. "Prepare to travel to the facility. You will *personally* complete the process by the end of the solar week. Captain Seonaid will be there."

The general broke the communication, leaving the doctor staring at a plain white screen. He hadn't liked this situation from the beginning, and he liked it even less now. There was more than a whiff of coercion.

He refused to start the process without hearing from the woman's lips that this was what she wanted.

General Seonaid cursed low and viciously under his breath. The bitch. The conniving *bitch*. She'd been a thorn in his side since the day she was born, emerging squalling from her mother's loins.

She had talent, was an exemplary soldier, yet she balked at this final step that would make her the perfect specimen.

A perfect *male* soldier.

His two oldest sons were doing well but didn't possess the same natural talent *she* displayed.

He snarled another pithy curse and rose to get a drink. Damn bitch. She was driving him to drink. She dared to make him appear stupid to his subordinates! He swallowed the liquor in one gulp, savoring the burn as it rushed down his throat.

General Seonaid returned to his desk and buzzed for his aide. He settled his bulk back onto his chair and checked his schedule. Nothing this morning. He'd make a surprise visit home and prize his daughter away from her aunt. And he'd make it very clear she *would* go to the medical center.

If she didn't, he'd force her to obey, no matter what her objections.

He intended to become General of the Army ahead of his friend and competition, General Gallagher. They might've gone to the academy together and entered into a friendly contest of one-upmanship, which had continued for most of their lives, but this was an instance in which he intended to gain the advantage.

Three successful sons would trump two, especially since he had two captains and a first lieutenant in *his* family, and a wife who supported him to the hilt. The perfect hostess when he needed to arrange a party for visiting dignitaries.

No, he'd beat Gallagher this time with his skill, his natural talent and his offspring. The top brass would like what he could bring to the position.

The title of General of the Army was his for the taking.

CHAPTER EIGHT

Felix and Gus made good time, urged on by cantankerous kittens that made no secret of their hatred for their cage. It seemed easier to keep traveling for as long as they could. The result was they trotted into the village hours earlier than expected.

Gus called out, which started the kittens crying. Alarm glittered on his face, his head whipping around to check on the tiny creatures.

Felix couldn't help grinning at the man's obvious panic, and he took off his shirt and draped it over the cat carrier. Immediately, the kittens quieted, and Gus muttered what sounded like a heartfelt thanks.

He led the way to a large stone building and spoke to two guards at the door. They stood aside and waved Gus and Felix inside.

"Felix!" Casey said. "That was quick."

Felix crossed the distance between them with long strides and seized Casey, hauling her into his arms. He crushed his mouth to hers and kissed her hard. When he lifted his head, he was breathing hard. She was leaning into him, and he welcomed her weight. "I missed you, sweetheart. What...what are you wearing?"

"One of the chief's wives lent me something clean to wear. Did you have any problems?"

He ran a quick finger along the neckline of the bright-pink fabric that was wrapped around her body like a sarong. "Not a one. We brought two kittens. I hope that will be sufficient to appease the chief."

"I'm sure it will," Casey said. "Come and meet the chief. I think you'll like him."

"The man intended to attack the resort," Felix growled. "I doubt I'll trust him."

"His senior warriors were a bit rigorous in interpreting the chief's wishes. Evidently the chief's daughter is popular. They like to please her."

Casey led him into an even larger room and paused to bow and wait for instructions to approach the throne. At least that's what Felix intimated from the words and actions. Interestingly enough, the stench he'd almost become used to wasn't present in here. Large urns of flowers stood near the throne, and their scent subtly perfumed the air.

Figuring he should copy Casey, Felix bowed and waited at her side while she addressed the chief. He studied the man—a mountain of green flesh with gold swirls cutting through the drab color of his skin. An explosion of dreads covered his head. His chest was broad, his biceps and triceps bulky with muscle. A man didn't get that way by lazing around and issuing orders.

Felix stood a little straighter, misgivings stirring in his gut. This situation had the potential to explode and have lasting repercussions if he didn't handle everything right. What would Saber do?

Felix thought about his brother, weighed the alternatives then formulated his plan. He'd study and listen before he acted. Gather the facts. Probably not the way his older brother would handle the situation, but Felix deemed his more cautious approach prudent. Putting Casey in danger wasn't an option.

Casey finished speaking, and Felix studied the chief's serious face, watching for any hint of the man's thoughts. His gaze met Felix's, and the chief inclined his head in recognition. He said something to Casey, and color appeared on her cheeks. She stammered back a reply.

Gus entered the room carrying the kittens. He, too, paused and bowed his head. One of the kittens let out a loud meow, and the sudden silence in the room grew deafening.

The chief gestured imperiously, added a command, and Gus scurried forward, careful of his cargo.

"He wants us to approach too," Casey said in a low voice. "He seems pleased."

Felix slipped his arm around Casey's shoulders and ushered her forward. *Yeah, you want to make sure the chief and every other male knows she belongs to you.*

Felix snorted inwardly at his thoughts. Casey belonged to him, belonged *with* him. She just didn't know it yet.

Gus set the cat carrier down and opened the door to lift out the ginger kitten. He stroked its head until it purred and spoke to the chief before handing him the animal.

The kitten seemed dwarfed in the chief's big hands, but Felix relaxed when the chief patted it with gentle fingers. Immediately the kitten started purring, and the chief gave a delighted chuckle. Gus handed him the black-and-white kitten, and the chief lifted his big round head and beamed at Felix and Casey.

He said something to Felix, and Casey interpreted.

"He wants to know how much you want to charge for the kittens."

Sweet Jesus. The man had ordered his men to steal a cat—one of his people—and now he wanted to pay for kittens? Felix kept his expression neutral with difficulty, finally gave up and forced his mouth to shape into a polite smile instead of the snarl of fury that trembled on the tip of his tongue. "Tell him the kittens are a gift, a peace offering to help foster a friendly relationship between our people."

Casey gave an imperceptible nod, and her eyes glowed with approval before she turned to face the chief and passed on Felix's words.

The chief said something else, and Casey laughed.

What now? Felix waited for Casey to let him in on the joke and mentally reinforced his plan to make upgrading their implants a priority.

"The chief asked if we have more we could give them in exchange for precious stones. He says his five wives will all want one too."

"Tell him I will speak to Jaycee and the other cat owners. They might wish to sell some of the offspring if there are more litters. We could let him know."

Casey and the chief had yet another conversation, a long and involved one. Felix scrutinized the man, yet he was difficult to read.

"The chief is surprised you allow your people to receive the payments. He thinks you're an honorable man and wishes to invite us to stay to celebrate his daughter's birth anniversary."

No, they needed to get back to the resort. With Saber away, he needed to be there in case of any problems. "Tell the chief I am honored by his invitation, but this time, I must leave immediately to return to my people because they will be worried about our absence. Please also tell him I would be further honored if he would like to visit my family at the resort. Perhaps by then, I'll know if we can expect more kittens."

Felix paused and cast a quick look at the chief. "Can you ask him—politely—if he could send word of his visit next time, so

SHELLEY MUNRO

we might prepare and greet him with proper ceremony? We don't want his warriors cutting their way into the resort. Suggest they come to the gate and ask for me or Saber, my older brother."

Casey smiled with approval. "Very tactful."

"I try," Felix said.

Despite Felix's impatience to leave, he and Casey shared a meal with the chief and his wives. The chief led them to yet another room. The scent of roast meat wafted through the air, and the chief beamed as he introduced his wives with Casey's aid. The chief strode to the head of the table and settled his weight on a bench before waving them to take the places of honor on either side of him. Several warriors filled the rest of the chairs at the table while two young girls handed around stoneware mugs filled with a mystery beverage.

Felix sipped cautiously and found the taste a little like beer. Not bad, but he made himself drink at a conservative pace. No telling how much of a kick the brew would give to the unwary imbiber.

Several women carried in platters of food and set them on the long table. Felix had worried about what they might be offered to eat, but the plates appeared to hold roasted birds about the size of an Earth turkey. A selection of pink tubers surrounded the birds, and another platter held a green leafy vegetable, which reminded him of spinach. His stomach rumbled, but he didn't think anyone noticed over the loud chatter.

So, they'd eat a meal, have a few drinks, and be on their way. He'd feel better once they arrived back at the resort.

"Time to go," Felix said. "Will you make our excuses to the chief?"

"Can't we stay overnight?" She'd had a day to think about her dilemma and had admitted with a heavy heart that it wouldn't be as easy as simply going AWOL. The general would search for her.

She should have reported to the medical center by now. Someone would have notified the general, and the military police would arrive at the resort soon. But if she wasn't there—

Scurvy sky pirates! Their next step would be to check her tracker chip. Every soldier on active duty had a chip. The fact she was retired meant tracking her was illegal—but that wouldn't stop the general.

Finnian bat crap. No matter what she did, she was doomed.

Felix rose and bent in a dignified bow toward the chief. "I want to get back to the resort. Saber is counting on me."

"Your man want to go?" the chief asked, a cheerful smile on his lips and a hint of a leer in his golden-brown eyes. At least Felix's presence had stopped the chief from demanding she join his herd of wives.

"Yes, he has responsibilities back at his home."

"He is a good man?"

"Yes." She didn't hesitate. Felix was a special man.

"You go then, but you come back to visit soon. My wives, they like you. Say they don't mind if you move into wives' house. Your man not treat you right, you come to me. I look after you."

Casey bowed her head and blinked to stall the burning at her eyes from blooming into weeping. All her life, apart from her aunt, she'd been alone, and now she had two men who wanted her. Pressure built in her chest, and she gave a short, hard laugh to dispel the tight sensation. "Thank you, Chief, but I like Felix."

He waved his green hand in a dismissive nature. "No matter. Offer stands."

"Thank you." Casey stood.

"You send message if you have more cats ready. I buy with stones."

"We will." She bowed again.

"You ask Gus for stinky ointment. Keep jungle bugs away," the chief said.

"Ah." Casey wrinkled her nose. "I will."

"Gus, Casey requires some stinky ointment and food for their journey," the chief shouted down the table.

Gus bounded to his feet and trotted off.

"Let's go," Casey said, her heart heavy.

"What's wrong?" Felix asked in an undertone. "Did the chief say something to upset you?"

Casey forced another smile and did a better job pulling it off this time. "He said if I wanted, I could stay here and move in with his wives."

Felix growled, and some of the boisterous chatter faded.

"I declined," she said hastily.

"Glad to hear it," Felix snapped. "We're going now." His hand curled around her upper arm, and with a final respectful bob, Felix propelled her from the chief's dining room.

"Gus is getting us food for our journey and some stinky ointment."

"No thank you on the ointment. I'd rather put up with the bugs," Felix said.

Gus arrived with a woven bag and two water bottles. He handed over a sealed stone jar. "This is ointment. I help you apply."

Felix growled again, and Gus gave a delighted laugh. He raised his hands and danced out of reach. "I see again."

"There's no need to act like a jealous lover."

"I don't like any man touching you. I *am* your lover," Felix gritted out. "Let's go. I want to get a good start before darkness falls."

Sighing, Casey fell in behind Felix. Every unwilling step took her closer to the resort and nearer to her future. She plodded along the trail and entered the muggy jungle.

It wasn't right for the general to order her to do this.

Not right. Not right. *Not right.*

Maybe she could file a complaint. No. The general would punish her and accuse her of airing family problems. Gods, no matter what she did, she couldn't win.

"I can hear you thinking. You're glaring holes in my back." Felix kept walking.

"I didn't want to leave yet."

Felix stopped and turned to glare at her. "Too bad. I wasn't leaving you there, not on your own. I've just found you, Casey. I don't want to lose you."

"But you don't own me."

Felix snorted and started striding through the jungle again. Birds sang, and bright-red insects kept landing on her bare shoulders and arms and legs. "*Scurvy sky pirates!* I hate these bugs." She slapped at them, the *smack, smack, smack,* and her loud complaints silencing the birds for a short time.

The heat was heavy, smothering her, thickening the air, and dragging sweat from her pores. The perspiration ran down her face, between her breasts and crawled down her spine. All this suffering and what would come at the end of it? The military police would arrive and drag her away. It wouldn't even surprise her if they were already at the resort. They'd take her away in handcuffs on the order of the general.

No. Not handcuffs. That might cause gossip. Her arrest would proceed in a civilized manner.

She cursed under her breath, angry at the general—the man who should be her protector—angry at the situation, angry at herself because she couldn't think of a way to avoid the inevitable.

Hours passed, and the sky—whenever she caught sight of it through gaps in the jungle—darkened, and different birds and insects came out to play. The red biting bugs vanished, only to be replaced by vibrant pink ones. They were smaller but nipped just as hard. "I'm tempted to break out the bug ointment."

Felix slowed. "Please don't," he said. "Once we get out of the jungle, there won't be as many bugs. There's a swimming hole with a waterfall. We can swim and cool off. Refresh." His eyes turned eerie green, the color shift that occurred when his feline half exerted his presence, she now realized. "Make love."

"Is sex all you think about?" The general might pounce at any moment. She stomped past Felix in an attempt to outrun the turmoil in her mind.

Felix grabbed her arm and hauled her to a halt. "What is wrong with you? You've looked like a thundercloud ever since we left the village."

"What's a thundercloud?" *All right.* Even *she* could hear the sulkiness coloring her tone. She sucked in a quick breath, placed her hand on her chest, and rubbed in an attempt to ease the heartache.

"You're grumpy. Why?"

He didn't intend to ease up this time. It was stamped on his features. Casey rubbed her chest again. The ache intensified instead of receding. The tight sensation crawled up her throat. She swallowed. Opened her mouth to refute him. Swallowed again.

"Casey." He shook her a little. "Tell me what's wrong. It's eating you up inside."

"I'm absent without leave," she said, and the tears finally spilled over, running down her cheeks. "Never mind. This waterhole. Which direction?"

"It's not your fault."

"The military won't see it that way," she snapped. "They think in black and white."

"We can explain," Felix said.

"Won't matter. The general will order a punishment." Of that she was sure. He wouldn't like his precious schedule thrown off.

"Your father?"

"Yes, the general. Now, if you don't mind, the waterhole…" she prompted, her tone a shade shy of nasty.

"Keep following the trail. There's a colony of bat-birds up ahead. Try not to startle them because they shit in self-defense. Gus thought it was funny."

Casey didn't answer, the pain in her chest growing with each step closer to the resort. They would've tried her communicator first. It was sitting in Felix's suite. Then they'd contact her family—in this case, the general. *He* would've contacted the family home to discover if she were there. He might call Aunt Elsa, maybe her brothers, despite them not being close. Then, once he'd ordered his aide to do all that, he would assume the worst and initialize tracking protocol.

She'd have to keep an eye skyward once they exited the jungle. The new stealth ships made no sound, and they could either take her out or snatch her in their retrieval beam if they had a clear sighting.

They wouldn't care about Felix. If he were injured or, worse, died while they were retrieving her, top brass would see his loss as that of necessary casualty.

Casey felt her mouth twist into a grimace. Of course, if they discovered he had a dual nature, they might consider him suitable to recruit. It wouldn't be voluntary. No, in this case, they'd snatch him up and force him into service. She'd seen it before, and the abuse of power sickened her to the soul.

She couldn't allow them to haul Felix or his siblings away.

It was better if she severed ties and ignored the way she felt about Felix. And best she start now, even though it made the pain in her chest spread.

She'd act the bitchy female, be generally annoying, and as soon as they arrived back at the resort, she'd board the first shuttle she could. Even a cargo shuttle, if that was all she could get. The sooner she put distance between herself and the people she'd come to love, the safer it would be for all concerned.

"It's my duty to return to service. I made a commitment to the military. You understand commitment and duty, Felix?" *Aw, low blow.* "I'll contact command on our return and request a personal interview with the general to explain the situation."

Like that was going to happen. She didn't intend to make this easy for the general. She'd request more time, more information. Attempt to stall in a last-ditch effort to make the general see reason because *she didn't want this.*

Acceding to the general's command would make her miserable. Oh, they might wipe her memories, even give her new ones in the process; they might make her stronger, they might make her bigger, but they couldn't give her love and respect.

Although she knew she wouldn't win, she had to try. For the first time in her life, she had to take a firm stand against the general.

Temper pumped through his veins. *No way.* No way did he intend to lose Casey now that he'd found her. He glared at her slim back as she plunged through the jungle in front of him. She was his mate.

Mine, his feline roared.

Felix's steps lengthened to keep up with her. She was practically running now, feet thudding the ground and breaking sticks, crackling leaves beneath her feet in the growing darkness. His eyesight was good in the dark, but Casey didn't have the same night vision.

She tripped, cursed, and picked herself up before he could offer his help. He hung back but watched her to make sure she didn't blunder into danger. Anything more dangerous than the bat-birds. They'd heard her coming, and he could hear their agitated chirps. A couple of them were already dropping their loads. He could smell the indescribable stench.

"Casey, you need to go slower."

"I don't have to do anything."

Was it his imagination, or was she crying again? Generally he gave weeping women a wide berth, but something was eating

Casey alive. To get to the rank of captain, she would've seen a lot of active service. She was tough—both mentally and physically. Yet she'd cried a lot since he'd known her. She'd had that stress attack at the capture compound. She didn't sleep, didn't eat much either.

Yeah, he agreed with his mother. Casey was suffering from severe stress, but what was causing it?

Her last mission?

Or something else?

Felix moved with caution since he didn't want to get covered with bat-bird crap again. At this pace, they'd get to the swimming hole in under an hour. They could use the same shelter he and Gus had built. Make use of their time in a more productive manner.

He'd worm the truth out of her somehow. Because he couldn't fix something he didn't know about.

Casey needed fixing, and he was the man to do the mending.

Mine, his feline growled.

Ours, Felix agreed, and his feline stretched beneath his skin.

Up ahead, Casey stumbled. A bat-bird let out its eerie shriek—a combo between a high-pitch squawk and a sonar beep.

Casey picked herself up and let out a sharp curse.

"Casey..." he warned.

Casey shrieked and gave a disgusted shout. "What was that?"

"Don't make any noise, and maybe the bat-birds will settle." Low chance, but maybe it would quiet her anger.

Casey stopped, allowing him to catch up. "I thought you were making that up," she whispered.

Felix wanted to laugh and would have if the stench didn't make his eyes water. Pale-blue poop covered her hair, dripped over her forehead, and trickled down to her chin. He composed himself with difficulty. "I don't lie to you."

Not quite true, but she wasn't exactly being forthcoming with him either. He figured that made them even.

"How much farther to the swimming hole?"

"Maybe half an hour."

She gave a tiny groan, and he grinned.

"Want me to lead?"

"Please."

He slipped past her and took the lead, taking care of his foot placement. The bat-birds were all awake now, making anxious noises in the trees above their heads. Casey was having difficulty seeing and kept stomping on sticks, making noises.

"*Scurvy sky pirates!*" she shrieked. "Go faster! Ugh, this is even more disgusting than the stink ointment. Aw, crap!" She groaned at another foul strike.

Felix knew better than to stand still. The rest of the colony would crap in sympathy the more nervous they got. He kept moving at a fast pace until he was out of range. Once there, he halted to wait for Casey.

His lips twitched upon seeing her. Crap covered her shoulders and most of the sarong the village women had given her. His nose bore the brunt of the assault, and he pinched it between finger and thumb.

"Funny," she gritted out. "Keep moving. I want to wash."

"Yes, ma'am."

She snarled, and a chuckle escaped him. At least she was worrying more about the crap than whatever was troubling her. Maybe this was a good thing.

He started walking, and she stumbled after him.

"I can't see a damn thing," she muttered.

He slowed. "It's not too far. Put your hand in the waistband of my trousers. I'll stop if there's a problem."

"Thanks," she said.

Her cool fingers sliding beneath the waistband of his trousers gave him a jolt. His feline twisted, sensing her proximity. Soon, he promised. *Soon.*

They walked in silence, Felix turning over the pieces of the Casey puzzle in his mind.

The tangle of trees and plants started to thin, and Felix heard the bubble of the stream that flowed into the swimming hole Gus had shown him. "Not far," he said.

"I've visited a lot of planets," Casey said. "But I have never suffered from such bad body odor before I came to Ione."

"Me either," Felix said and didn't attempt to smother his amusement. "Tiraq comes with challenges." He came to a halt at a spot where a stream crossed the trail. "You'd better wash off the worst of the bat-bird crap in the stream here. We don't want to foul the water in the pool, which is upstream a bit to our left. If you go to the right, the water is hip-deep a bit farther along."

"Very funny. Didn't you get hit?"

"Not this time. I did on the journey to the village."

Casey muttered under her breath, and Felix watched her stumble into the middle of the stream and start scrubbing at her skin. She ducked her head right under the water and came up spluttering. "It's colder than I thought it would be."

"Cold or clean?"

"Like I said. Funny man." She continued washing and removed her sarong to rub the fabric against a rock that jutted out from the water. "There," she said after another five minutes. "That should do it."

She waded out of the stream, water dripping off her hair. She shivered.

"It's not far to the pool. Part of it is warmer. A hot spring, Gus said."

"*Now* you tell me," Casey complained.

"I thought a big tough soldier like you could cope with anything?"

She froze, all expression sliding off her face, and Felix kicked himself.

No, damn it! He was tired of tiptoeing around her problems.

After they'd swum and warmed up, they'd slip into the shelter and make love. Once he'd helped her relax, he'd ask the hard questions and expect her to answer.

Time for them both to face the truth.

They were meant to stay together, and nothing could stop it from happening while he still had breath in his body.

Felix stopped by the shelter and dropped the bag of provisions the villagers had given them. Casey's clothes were packed in the top, so at least she'd have dry clothes for the morning. He stripped off his boots and clothing.

Casey waited beside him and followed him to the pool's edge.

"It'll be cold at first. The warm spot is over on the other side."

Casey seemed to cheer up a bit once they got warm. They splashed and laughed until exhausted, then they let the warm water soothe them.

"Is this the only warm spot?"

"So Gus indicated," Felix said. "I think the water cools quickly once it runs out of the pool. Difficult to know for sure since we couldn't communicate with words, but we got good at sign language. Are you ready to get out?"

"I feel clean again, and I can't smell that disgusting bird crap any longer."

"Memorable, isn't it?"

"Yes."

If the military police were on their way, this was Casey's last night with Felix. Against her better judgment, instead of sniping at him, she should enjoy the time they had left. Now that the lunar-moon had come out, she could see the glint in his eyes, knew what it meant. He wanted to have sex.

Make love, her innermost self corrected.

While there were lots of reasons for her to resist, she wasn't going to.

118

Make memories. Savor them while they last.

She followed him to the shelter, shivering in the breeze.

"In you go," he said.

"Have you checked for visitors?"

"There aren't any. I'd smell them, hear them. The shelter is clear."

"I'll take your word for it and take it out on your hide if you're wrong."

"Sounds kinky, but maybe you shouldn't give me ideas," he said in a low growl. "I owe you a spanking for not staying out of danger."

Casey twisted to stare at him. "What? I helped saved Mitchell butt by going with them. The skirmish could have turned nasty if it weren't for me."

"Not the point. I made a promise, and I *will* deliver."

Hadn't she promised the general she'd go through with the nanotechnology?

Not the same, her mind screeched. *Not the same at all.*

Her shoulders sagged. If he spanked her, so be it. Something else to remember about Felix—his penchant for spanking.

Casey crawled into the dark shelter. There wasn't much room, but at least she was out of the cool breeze. The dried leaves cushioned her body. Not too bad.

Felix joined her and drew her into his arms. She smelled his masculine scent and the greenery surrounding them and sighed. Safety felt like this, had the same aroma.

He kissed her, and she murmured against his mouth. She had no idea what she was trying to say, but she savored the easy thrust of his tongue into her mouth. The taste of him swept over her, familiar now. She burrowed her fingers into his hair, gripped hard in a silent demand to take the contact deeper, faster.

Already she felt the swell of his erection against her hip. The instant he'd touched her, her body had softened, readying for his possession. Her breasts swelled, her nipples hardening to taut points against his chest.

"Now," she demanded.

"You've missed this as much as I have." Satisfaction throbbed in his voice, a hint of smugness.

"No. You're good though. You know how to play a woman's body."

"Careful," he answered in a silky tone. "It's not too late to spank the lies out of you."

"We don't have a future, Felix."

"Bullshit," he snarled.

Casey didn't know what bulls or their crap had to do with the situation, but she recognized the dangerous edge to his tone. She pressed a kiss to his shoulder, licked across his collarbone and nipped at the soft patch of skin where shoulder and neck met.

He let out a snarl—a feline snarl—and Casey froze, unsure of what she'd done.

He rolled her under him, crushed her mouth to his, and this time, he didn't muck around. He fucked her mouth with his tongue, pulled a tortured groan from her then did it all over again.

With his thigh, he parted her legs, his fingers dancing over her folds, teasing her clit while he settled in at her breast. He tugged her nipple between his teeth, sucked hard, bit lightly until her head spun and her fingernails dug into his shoulders.

"Please, Felix. Please."

"Please what?" he asked hoarsely.

"Fuck me. Take me now."

He exploded into action, guiding his cock to her opening and pushing deep with one hard thrust. Casey groaned, stunned by the way this situation had spun out of control yet desperate for him to take her and make her come hard enough to push away every single thought.

His strokes were forceful, his breath hot against her cheek. His tongue rasped across the same place she'd teased at *his* neck, and the abrasive sensation sent a shudder of pleasure coursing through her body. Gods, he was good at this. So, so good. He made her feel invincible as if she were flying.

He continued to tease the spot on her neck, the skin becoming tender. Casey jolted when he gave her a hint of teeth. He slipped a hand between her legs and rubbed her clit. Another surge of pleasure struck, and Casey moaned.

"Yes," she cried out. "Yes, yes!"

He plunged deep and bit down.

It was too much. Not enough. She cried out once more.

Felix bit her again, harder this time.

Pain filled her, collided with the pleasure—and then she was tearing apart at the seams, coming so hard she wondered if the ecstasy would make her pass out. She was aware of Felix's shout, the convulsive heave of his body as he climaxed.

Gradually, gradually, she came back, her body loose and relaxed. Felix licked a spot high on her shoulder, and she was aware of a lingering soreness. She trembled, and her pussy gave a spasm, tightening around his cock.

Casey yawned. "That was amazing. I don't think I've ever come that hard before."

"Told you I was good."

"Big head."

Felix just grinned and gathered her close. Before she knew it, she was asleep.

CHAPTER NINE

General Seonaid buzzed his aide. Three quick stabs of his finger before the skinny Palito man scuttled through the door connecting their offices. His off-white eyes protruded, and he couldn't stand still or maintain a gaze. Buggy in appearance *and* behavior. *Imbecile.*

"Yes, sir?" He saluted in the respectful way the general expected from his subordinates.

"Have you located Captain Seonaid?"

"No, sir."

The general tapped his fingers on his desktop and frowned. "Why not?"

"She's not answering her com-circle, sir. No one has seen her on Dalcon, and she's not at the resort where she was booked during her leave."

The general tapped his fingers again, a loud drumroll of

impatience. Damn the woman. She'd always been trouble, never did what was required of her. She always had to ask questions. Questions, questions, questions, until he lost patience.

"Take steps to track her via her chip," the general barked.

"But sir, Captain Seonaid has been discharged from the military. It would be against the law to track her."

"I'll authorize it," the general snarled.

"Sir, the reconnaissance department won't do it straight away. They are working on the space pirates plaguing the north sector of the galaxy."

The general picked up a glossy black-and-red stone, one mined on the planet Dalcon. He tossed it from hand to hand even as he narrowed his gaze on his aide. "You tell them to give this priority. Find Captain Seonaid. She has a health condition and must enter the medical facility immediately."

"Her records don't state she suffers from a medical condition."

Annoying bug. "She caught a virus during her last mission but refuses to accept she's dying. We—my wife and sons—are worried about her." The general lied without a qualm and even squeezed his features into sadness.

"I'm sorry to hear that, sir. I'll contact reconnaissance right now."

The general sighed and set the black-and-red rock down on his desktop. It clicked loudly in the silence. "Thank you."

The general waited until his aide exited the office and shut the connecting door behind him. He stood and made his way to the window, which overlooked the city and the palace in the distance. Only then did he allow a slow smile to curl his lips.

They would find Casey, and when they did, he'd get his way. He'd lose a daughter and gain a son, and that promotion would bear his name.

"We should go," Casey said.

"Soon," Felix replied with a lazy yawn. He rolled, pinning her beneath his weight. "I think we have time for a bit of canoodling."

"Exactly what is canoodling?"

He grinned. No, it was more of a smirk.

"It means I get to kiss you some more and make love to you again."

"But I need to get back to the resort."

"Wrong answer," he said and trailed a line of kisses down her jawline, down her throat, down to the spot where he'd bitten her at the height of passion last night. She expected pain because he'd bitten hard, but instead, a surge of sensual energy flashed through her body.

She gulped and shuddered when his fingers traced across the same spot. Sensations ripped through her, too fast, too many to catalog. Startled, she glanced at him and saw the way his eyes widened.

"What?"

"I...ah..." He gestured at her neck. "There's a mark where I bit you. I'm sorry. I didn't mean to hurt you."

"Of course there are teeth marks. You bit me. It doesn't hurt though."

Felix's brows drew together, confusion and wonder combining on his face. "Can you see it?"

"No, not properly. Tell me, what is it?"

"There's a...a tattoo where I bit you—a small black cat." He fingered the spot, and a groan burst from her throat.

"*Scurvy sky pirates*," she muttered. "Every time you stroke me there, I feel it down here." She cupped her sex.

"Works for me," he said, his slow smile making her want to grin in return.

He linked their fingers and nuzzled her neck, taking tiny bites from her throat. The instant his mouth came into contact with *the* spot, she sucked in a wildly excited breath. The seductive stroke of his tongue forced another cry from her, desire kicking her in the belly.

No longer did she want to leave. No, she was weak. A few kisses, a few touches, and she wanted to linger to enjoy every minute. A heavy pulsating sensation filled her pussy as he kissed her again.

"Spread your legs for me, sweetheart."

The endearment had her obeying. His finger lightly circled her clit, and her heart thundered as if she were running a race. He traced her slit with a gentle finger then lifted her to his mouth to give her a pleasuring stroke across her swollen flesh. Talk about sweet agony. No, she didn't want to leave now.

She gripped his hair, holding his face in place.

"More, more, more," she chanted.

His tongue was rough against her clit. It was abrasive and sexy and pushed her into a place of raw need.

"Let go, sweetheart."

"No, I want...I need..." She tugged his hair harder and lifted her hips to gain more pressure from his mouth.

"I'm not going to stop. Promise. I'm going to fill you, give us both pleasure."

She released her grip enough for him to move over her. He manacled her wrists with his hands and licked around one nipple.

"You promised," she said. "Please. Please put your cock inside me."

Felix laughed and continued to tease her, driving her higher, faster, harder. She felt the slickness of her pussy, felt the throb of her clitoris, felt the surge of heat when he licked across the tattoo.

Her channel gave a spasm, and she groaned with disappointment.

Felix smiled, pressed a lingering kiss to her lips, and then put his cock exactly where she wanted it. He drove into her and shoved her past the point of no return.

Gods, how would she ever walk away with her heart intact?

She gasped for air, cradled his big body against hers and tried not to cry. She already knew the answer.

She wouldn't.

When she walked away to keep Felix and his family safe from the general's ire, she'd leave her heart behind.

A day later, Felix was pleased to note someone had taken care of repairs to the fence. He also picked up the subtle hum of the silent alarm, doing its job of protecting the perimeter. No more blaring sirens throughout the resort in the middle of the night.

"We'll go via the rear entrance and head straight to my suite. That way, we can clean up before we meet anyone."

Casey gave an abrupt nod. "Okay."

Felix's feline stirred with a cranky snarl. He shot a glance at Casey, noting her unhappiness. The closer they'd gotten to the resort, the quieter she'd become. And she was still insisting she was returning to Dalcon on the next available shuttle.

He begged to differ.

No way. No how. Not in his lifetime.

She wasn't going anywhere without him at her side.

They made it to his suite without bumping into anyone. Felix pressed his palm against the door pad and the locks disengaged. He opened the door and stood back for Casey to enter.

"I'm going to check in with Ma and my brothers," he said. "You use the sanitizer room first."

She gave another clipped nod and disappeared. For a

nanosecond, he was tempted to follow her and demand answers, to tell her how their future would work. Together. He didn't. Instead, he left his suite and went to find his mother.

He found her in the resort office, in the center of a ring of male employees. Everyone was talking at once. Scarlett watched warily from her desk on the far side of the room, and their secretary-receptionist looked as if she wanted to flee the melee.

"It's not fair," Laurence said. "Justin gets to work in the holo room. He gets all the women. I'm stuck at the shuttle port."

"It's not my fault," Justin said and shoved Laurence.

Laurence shoved back.

"I don't want to work in the back office," another man protested.

"The roster isn't fair," a younger male shouted.

Felix waded through the crowd and halted by his mother. "That's enough," he snapped. "You will give your name to Scarlett, give her a brief description of your complaint, and she will organize a time for each of you to speak with me and air your grievances. Once I have a full picture, I will take action to sort out this mess. Understand?"

When no one said a word, he nodded. "Right. Form a line, give your details to Scarlett and return to your assigned posts."

Laurence stalked over to Scarlett's desk and murmured a few words before wheeling around. "If things don't improve around here, there's gonna be trouble."

Felix scowled after the retreating man. "I really don't like him."

"Shush, son. He's still grieving his sister's death."

"Sure, Ma, but how long do we tiptoe around his feelings? Lots of us lost friends and family after the virus outbreak. He doesn't have an exclusive on grief," Felix said.

"I'm glad you arrived when you did." Anna patted his arm. "Things were getting nasty."

"Anything else I should know about?"

"I have a list," she said drily. "Someone is still cutting holes in the perimeter fence. One of the holo rooms is out of action because someone vandalized the control center. Also we seem to have a thief. I don't know if it's a guest or a staff member, but either way, it's not good publicity. Oh, and someone from the military is trying to contact Casey. I told them she wasn't here, but they were very insistent."

Foreboding went through Felix, but he bit it back. Casey was safe in his suite. "Okay, Ma. Let's go through the problems one at a time and try to make sense of them." He urged his mother into Saber's office and closed the door.

They were halfway through the list when his com-circle buzzed.

"Felix," he said, his mind on the thefts. He and his brothers worked long hours now. They didn't need to spend half their nights prowling the resort under the guise of security.

"It's Saber. Can you meet me at the shuttle port and fuel up another shuttle for me to fly to Dalcon? I'll be there in half an hour."

"But what—" The com cut off before he could get out his question. "Saber's back."

"Oh good," Anna said. "I can't wait to see him."

"It doesn't sound as if he intends to stay," Felix said. "I'd better fuel a shuttle."

When Saber landed the craft on the shuttle pad, Felix was waiting for him.

"Where the hell have you been?" Felix demanded. "Are you both okay?" His gaze went from Eva to a plump blue bird that was letting out anxious squawks. "What the hell is that?"

"Is the shuttle fueled?"

"Yeah," Felix said. "I got Laurence to take care of that for you."

"Thanks. We'd better go. I need someone to return this shuttle." Saber plucked the bird from Eva's arms and handed the honking thing to Felix. "This is Bluebird. Give him to Scarlett to look after."

"It's not dinner?" Felix asked.

"Bluebird is *not* dinner," Eva snapped. "And if I come back and discover Bluebird missing, I'll hunt you down."

A spurt of humor made his lips quirk upward, quickly controlled when he saw the promise to follow through glittering in her eyes. "Yes ma'am. When will you be back?"

"I'm not sure," Saber said. "A few days, maybe longer."

Great. In the past, he'd resented Saber, felt a bit like a useless spare wheel while his older brother plowed through life's challenges. Now that he was standing in Saber's shoes, he realized the hard and challenging line Saber walked. Yet his brother took everything in his stride.

It made Felix appreciate his big brother. Right then, he made a promise to himself that instead of fanning his resentment, he'd get off his backside and offer to take up some of the slack. "Contact Ma, will you? She's been worried about— *What the fuck?*"

The shuttle Saber and Eva had arrived in shimmered before his eyes and, bit by bit, faded away until nothing stood on the shuttle pad.

Saber strode to the pad and walked straight through the empty air. "Fuck, that's all kinds of disturbing."

Felix stared, wondering if he'd imagined the entire vessel.

"It's lucky we flew straight here," Eva said, her cheeks bleached of color. "What if it had disappeared while we were in flight? We could have d-died."

Saber went to her and pulled her against his chest. "We made it here in one piece, kitten." He stared over her head, his gaze connecting with Felix's before he closed his eyes.

Felix could tell what his brother was thinking. Hell, he felt the same way about Casey.

Eva pulled away from Saber and ran her hands down her body, patting the clothes she wore. Her expression was one of horror. "Do you think our clothes will vanish too?"

Felix barked out a laugh and did a quick visual sweep of his brother's mate even as he stroked the bird he was holding in an effort to calm the creature. "Could be quite a show." His gaze rose and snagged on a tiny tattoo on her upper shoulder, near her neck.

What the hell? That was the same as Casey's.

Saber let out a feral snarl and Felix straightened, wiping his expression clean. Obviously not the time to ask questions. Understanding the urge to protect a mate, Felix moved back half a step to show Saber he meant no harm to Eva.

Saber's growls subsided. "Your call," he said to Eva. "We can grab fresh clothes, but we'll lose time because my mother will want to meet you and feed us."

She swallowed. "Let's risk the clothes. Can't be worse than a cooking pot."

Wondering what the heck *that* meant, Felix stood back while Saber hustled Eva into the shuttle. He saw the way Saber placed a solicitous hand at the small of her back. Felix also noticed a softness to his brother's features that hadn't been present for a long time, as if he'd found what he was looking for after a long search. He saw contentment, and was pleased for Saber.

It made him even more determined to understand the reasons Casey was resisting him so hard.

Felix waited until the shuttle took off. The ridiculous blue bird, which looked like the offspring of the long-extinct dodo and a goose, didn't struggle but when he stopped stroking the bird's back, it let out anxious honk.

Laurence sidled closer, and Felix got a whiff of shuttle fuel. "Who was the woman with Saber?"

"Eva, Saber's mate." Felix shot Laurence a hard look. "Don't make trouble for him. He deserves some happiness."

"What about Lori?" Laurence snarled and his eyes shifted.

Felix growled back and advanced on him. Bluebird gave an anxious honk, but Felix didn't stop until his face was right in Laurence's. "You stay away from Saber. It wasn't his fault Lori died. We've all lost friends, loved ones. If I hear you mouthing off about his mate, you'll have *me* to deal with."

Laurence took a rapid step back, shifted his gaze and drooped into a submissive pose. Asshole. When Laurence didn't look at him again, Felix relaxed. He stroked the bird, waited a beat.

"I'll look into your complaints, along with the others."

Laurence gave a stiff nod and retreated.

Felix smoothed his hand over the bird's head and hurried off to find Scarlett and pass off his responsibility.

"Hey, Ma. Where's Scarlett?"

Anna grinned at the bird he carried under his arm. "She probably saw you coming. I take it you want her to look after the bird?"

"Yeah. Saber left it before he took off for Dalcon. He had Eva with him, and she threatened me with bodily harm if I didn't look after the bird."

"I like her already," Anna said. "Did Saber look happy?"

"Yeah, he did. I've never seen him look like this—not even with Lori." Felix paused. "Ma, do you know anything about a male biting a female and leaving a mark?"

Anna's eyes narrowed. "A mating mark? Why?"

"Tell me what you know. Please."

"Centuries ago, male shifters would bite their mates high on the shoulder. If a couple was compatible mates, the urge to bite would become so overwhelming the male didn't have any choice but to mark his mate. At least that's what I've learned from my research. I believe the original feline shifters who lived in New Zealand all mated this way, but somehow during the passing years, the urge has been lost. It didn't seem to make any difference to the way couples paired up, so the medical types didn't worry too much about the loss of the tradition. Now tell me why you want to know."

"Eva has one of these mating marks. It's not big, but it's shaped like a black cat."

"Really?" Interest sparked in Anna's eyes. "Did you ask Saber about it?"

Felix snorted. "He got edgy when I moved too close to Eva. I made a joke and he snarled at me, so I backed off and figured I'd talk to you."

"Interesting." Anna pursed her lips, obviously deep in thought. "How long has it been since the marks were evident?"

"I'll have to do some research, but my grandmother didn't have one. I don't know if David's mother had one. A cat, you say? *Very* interesting. Let me research my books." She picked her reader off the corner of her desk, and started tapping to bring up copies of her research books.

Felix rolled his eyes. And he'd lost her already. His mother kept the Mitchell genealogical records and had a vast collection of historical treatises that related to their settlement in New Zealand from Scotland. "Ma. Ma!"

"Yes, Felix?" she asked in an absent voice.

"There's something else. I bit Casey...and *she* has the same mark as Eva."

His mother's attention jerked from her reader, her eyes wide and full of wonder. Her lips curled into a teary smile. "Oh Felix. You too?"

Casey's com-circle was full of messages. Her stomach flipped, and she set the round unit down with a hard click. The messages could wait.

Clothes. She should pack and get ready to depart. She should leave today, before the general sent someone to retrieve her from the resort.

Her com buzzed, and she stared at it for an instant. No, not yet. She wasn't ready. Casey grabbed clothes at random and went to wash, perfectly aware she was putting off the inevitable.

Finally, after she'd packed, washed, and changed, she faced the fact she'd run out of excuses not to check her com-circle.

"Captain Seonaid, this is Owen Nelson, the general's aide. Please contact this office to reschedule your medical appointment."

Casey deleted the message.

"Captain Seonaid, this is the general's aide. He is most anxious for you to contact this office when you receive this message."

"Captain Seonaid, the general is worried about your health. You are not helping yourself by refusing to acknowledge my messages. Please contact me so medical assistance may be sought."

Delete. Delete. *Delete.*

"Captain Seonaid." Casey jerked at the sound of the general's voice barking through her com. "I insist you report to the medical facility for a meeting immediately. If you choose not to arrive for your appointment there will be consequences."

He couldn't even bring himself to call her by name. Casey deleted the rest of her messages without listening to them and slammed her com down.

A knock sounded on the door. "Casey, are you there?" Her aunt's voice came through the door, and Casey hurried to answer.

"Aunt Elsa." Casey didn't have to pretend pleasure at her aunt's visit. "I thought you might have gone back to Dalcon."

"No, Anna offered me a position here. I've decided to accept and relocate the business here, as we discussed." She shot her niece a concerned look. "What about you, dear? It looks as if you've packed to leave. Surely you're not following through with the general's wishes?"

Tears blurred her vision. "Aunt Elsa, what option do I have?"

"You can tell the general *no*! You can make his attempts to force you to undergo the process public knowledge. No man should have that much power. It's gone to his head. Besides, if you change from female to male, it won't make him love you more. He's cold and emotionless. Selfish. All he thinks of is himself and what suits *him*. Please, Casey. Don't do this."

"You don't understand," Casey said.

"Explain it to me then, Casey," Felix said from the open doorway. "Explain to me why you'd leave when we're meant to be together."

CHAPTER TEN

Felix stepped inside and shut the door, the sharp click sounding loud in the taut silence. "Casey," he prompted.

She cast a panicked glance at her aunt, received no encouragement from that quarter, and her shoulders rounded into a defensive slump. "The general is looking for me."

"Your father."

She gave a defeated nod.

"Understandable. Parents worry." Except maybe not hers. His feline stirred unhappily, and Felix stood ready to fight the invisible threat to his mate. "I thought we were past this. Explain to me why you feel you have to leave." He scowled at Casey's packed bags. "You intended to say goodbye, at least?"

A guilty flush suffused her cheeks, and a growl rumbled up his throat.

"Maybe you should go," he said to Elsa. "I won't hurt her."

"You spanked me," Casey blurted.

His brows rose. "I believe I explained why."

Elsa let out a sound, not quite a laugh. Her eyes twinkled. "Maybe I'll speak with Anna to discuss a new idea I've had for the boutique."

Felix didn't take his eyes off Casey. "I owe you another spanking. I haven't forgotten. This little stunt of yours might require more thought, though."

"I have a tracker. Felix, they know where to find me."

"Bloody hell." He straightened and glared at her. "Don't you think you should have informed me earlier?"

A sheen of moisture muted the color of her pretty eyes as she stared at him. "They won't stop until they retrieve me. Once the general gets irked enough, he'll send an extraction team. He will *not* give up until he gets what he wants." She sank down on the bed as if her legs could no longer hold her.

"What does he want?" Felix crossed the distance between them and crouched by her so he could see her face. "I don't think familial love is driving this need for your presence."

"Officially, I'm not in the military any longer. I received my discharge papers before I came to Tiraq."

"Okay." Felix didn't pretend to understand. "If you're no longer military, why would they bother sending an extraction team? Your family knows they can contact you via your com. They must know you came to the resort of your own volition." Felix thought a moment and scowled. "Your aunt knows."

"Yes," Casey whispered, and pain slid over her face. Misery.

Witnessing it hacked at Felix's bad mood, and his temper gave way to concern. "What the fuck could be so bad?"

She gave an audible swallow and a tear rolled down her face. Felix rose and lifted her, resettling himself on the end of the sleep-bed with her in his lap. She buried her face against his chest, her body quivering like treetops during a strong breeze.

Impatience pushed through him, propelled by his feline, but Felix waited and stroked her back in the same way he'd calmed Bluebird. Gradually, she settled, and the tremors ceased.

She met his gaze again, and her face flushed, a notable contrast to her dull, lifeless eyes. "The general has arranged an appointment at a military medical facility. He is insisting they carry out nanotechnology on me."

"For what? You're not sick. I'd sense it."

Her mouth twisted, anguish showing in every line and shadow on her face. "The general wants me to undergo new technology that will transform me from female to male."

Felix stared, his mouth dropping open. "A sex-change operation? In God's name, *why*? You're perfect as you are."

A laugh barked from Casey. Harsh and loud, it seemed to come from deep in her chest and claw its way free in an ugly burst. "The general wants another son. Once the operation is complete, he intends to welcome me to the world as Arthur Seonaid. Named after *him*, of course. He seems to think that three strapping sons, all of whom are successful and have achieved high rank within the military, will add to his prestige. He hopes to gain a promotion."

"But you're successful *now*." Felix was having trouble understanding the logic. His mate was perfect. Casey was gorgeous, intelligent and had already achieved success and rank. She was talented in design and a loving woman. How could that not be enough for a father? Fuck, what kind of parent would subject their child to this sort of emotional torment?

The low-level anger pumping through him ramped up to cold fury, but he never stopped stroking Casey, never stopped holding her, never stopped offering her comfort.

"I'm a female. No female has ever gone above the rank of captain."

"If you're no longer in the military, he can't force this experiment on you. What does your mother think? Your brothers?"

"I doubt anyone consulted my brothers, but my mother wouldn't care. She said the general knew what was best for us, and I should follow orders. She said I'd look striking in a military dress uniform, e-especially if...esp-especially if they f-fixed my-my face."

"There's nothing wrong with your face. You're gorgeous! You have pretty brown eyes that remind me of whiskey." He ran his fingers across her chin. "I like your determined chin and the way you lift it when you're trying to challenge me. I like your pert nose and these beautiful, sexy lips."

"My mother also doesn't like my hair."

"What's wrong with your hair? It's perfectly good hair."

"I cut it short because it was easier to look after and for safety reasons. If my hair is short, no one can grab me it in hand-to-hand combat."

"Hair is a trapping. Long, short or none at all. It doesn't define you, Casey. It's a person's heart that makes them special." He stroked her cheek and wiped away a tear. "You have a beautiful one. You're loving and display so much courage. You have integrity and tact. That was obvious in the way you dealt with the chief and his people. You're loyal and clever, and to me, you're beautiful. I intend to spend the rest of my life making you happy because being with you makes me happier than I can ever remember."

She gave him a misty smile, but it faded as her mind did an obvious flit. "The general is determined. He's already left me messages, telling me to present myself to the medical facility."

"What can he do if you refuse?"

"You don't understand. He *will* send an extraction team, and he won't care if anyone gets hurt. I need to go because I'd never forgive myself if you or your mother or siblings got injured because of my disagreement with the general."

It occurred to Felix she almost never referred to him as her father. It was always the general, and she seldom mentioned her mother or brothers. When she spoke of family, it was her aunt, and Felix gave silent thanks to the woman for trying to provide Casey with some sense of normality.

"This technology—will it wipe your personality?"

His hands tightened on her shoulders when she nodded.

Her wince had him forcing himself to relax and resume his stroking. "Sorry, sweetheart."

Essentially, the man was trying to obliterate his daughter, so nothing remained until he gained a precious son. Felix couldn't begin to understand, not when every child—male or female—held value within his world.

His mouth twisted when the irony struck him. They were attempting to steal females because they had a shortage, and the general wanted males. Kinda funny in a warped way.

"Tell me about this tracker you wear."

"It's here, beneath the skin." She fingered the back of her neck, toward her left shoulder. "They used to place them in the forearm, but some of the alien species we fight like to hack off arms and legs. The trackers would be lost, but the soldiers weren't necessarily dead. They were then placed in the current position."

"Very practical," Felix said. "Let me see." He felt the region of her shoulder she indicated, felt the tiny bump beneath her skin. "Right. We'll get rid of it. It's not deep." He scooped her off his knee and placed her on the sleep-bed. He pulled out his com-circle. "Scarlett, I need you in my suite. Casey has a tracker we need to get rid of."

He repeated the call to his other brothers then settled back to wait for them to arrive.

Scarlet arrived first and carried a bag. "Let's have a look at the tracker," she said, her tone brisk. "I might be able to jam it somehow."

Casey took off her shirt.

"What a cute cat tattoo," Scarlett said. "It's so tiny. When did you get it?"

"I bit her," Felix said. "The tracker."

Scarlett shot him an incredulous look, one that shouted clearly there *would* be questions, but she kept her curiosity contained. She ran her fingers over the spot on Casey's shoulders, hummed, and opened her bag. She pulled out several gadgets, making a *tutting* sound when she ran them over the tracker. "Hmm," she said.

On hearing a sharp knock, Felix rose to answer the door and let in Sly and Joe. Leo arrived a few minutes later.

"What's this about a tracker?" Leo asked.

Shock pelted Felix when he looked at his brother. He hadn't seen Leo for a few days, and he'd lost weight in that short time. There was a gray cast to his skin. Felix opened his mouth to ask questions but stopped when Joe elbowed him in the ribs.

"Casey has one in her shoulder. We need to neutralize or cut it out and destroy the bloody thing."

"It's going to need to be cut out," Scarlet said. "Nothing I have is strong enough to block the signal."

"It's transmitting?" Casey asked.

"Yes," Scarlet said. "Blocking wouldn't be a permanent solution anyway. It would only work if you stayed within range. The tracker would start transmitting again if you left the resort."

"Let me see," Leo said.

Felix struggled with his urge to growl when Leo placed his hand on Casey's shoulder.

"Can you move so you're under the light?" Leo asked.

Felix got a chair and motioned for Casey to sit in it. He spotted the exact moment his brothers noticed Casey's tattoo. His feline pushed out a warning growl, and his brothers moved carefully, keeping their gazes downward as they edged around Casey,

"Steady, bro," Scarlett said, squeezing his arm. "They're trying to help."

Felix took a deep breath and rounded the chair to face Casey.

He sat on the floor at her feet and soothed himself by pressing up against her leg. Only then did his brothers move more naturally.

"What do you think?" Leo asked Joe and Sly.

"You can feel it just below the surface. I think we should remove it," Sly said. "Use one of Ma's scalpels."

"Then destroy it," Felix said.

"No." A mischievous expression flooded Scarlett's face. "I think we should mail it to Earth. The pickup is in an hour. If we hurry, we could catch the mail shuttle. Think of all the stops it makes, all the sorting stations the package would go through before it arrives on Earth. We'll send it to my friend's post office box. If someone retrieves the package, it won't matter."

"I have to go to Dalcon today," Leo said. "I'll deliver it to the mailing office there so the package doesn't originate at the resort."

"They'll think I'm obeying orders and returning," Casey said.

"I like it," Felix said.

"I'll go get Ma's scalpel," Joe said.

"I'll go too and distract Ma," Sly said. "We don't want her demanding answers."

What none of his brothers or his sister mentioned were the possible legal repercussions, and Felix was grateful for their restraint. "Thanks."

Joe was back in mere minutes. Sly took a little longer to return, and Leo had already sprayed his hands and the tracker area with anti-germ.

"It's gonna hurt," Scarlett said.

"Do it," Casey whispered.

"I'll help," Felix said and rose to a kneeling position. He pressed a kiss to her lips and ran his finger over the marking site.

She moaned, jolted.

"Hold still," Leo said tersely.

"You can do this," Felix whispered and stroked the tattoo again. This time, she didn't move, but her eyes went soft as she locked her gaze with his.

"Got it," Leo said a few seconds later. "Fuck, she's bleeding a lot. Joe, hand me a pad from Ma's kit."

Felix kissed her and rose. "I've got it." He took the pad from Joe and pressed it to the wound.

Scarlett took the tracker from Leo. "I'll package it up. Better wash it first. Don't want the scent of blood anywhere near the package."

Felix lifted the pad and frowned at the instant beading of blood. His gut told him to lick the wound, so he followed instinct. He curled one hand around her other shoulder for balance, and when she gave a throaty moan, he knew he'd touched the tattoo. He continued to lazily stroke the spot while he bent his head and ran his tongue over the cut. The taste of her blood, coppery and so *her*, flooded his mouth. His eyes closed and he licked again and again until the bleeding slowed then ceased. When he lifted his head, the small wound was no longer open—only a bright-pink scar highlighted the spot.

"Amazing," Joe whispered. "How?"

Leo speared him a glance, curiosity a contrast to the shadows beneath his green eyes. "How did you know what to do?"

"What's wrong?" Casey asked.

"Nothing, sweetheart. I didn't. I listened to my gut," Felix said. "Maybe Ma will know. She said she's doing research."

"Ah," Sly said, a hint of laughter in his voice. "That would be why my distraction methods worked so easily. Her mind was on her diaries."

Leo sighed. "I'd better get moving. The shuttle will arrive soon. I'll take care of the package for you."

"Thanks," Felix said and gave his brother a swift hug. "That was a fine piece of work."

"You can return Ma's scalpel," Joe said. "Sly and I did the hard bit."

"Thanks." Felix hugged the twins too and escorted them to the door. He closed and locked it behind them before turning back to Casey. "You okay?"

"Tired," she said.

"Let's go to bed then. Ma will let me know if I'm needed." He urged her toward the sleep-bed and pulled back the covers.

"Do I need a dressing on my shoulder?"

"No, sweetheart. The wound healed after I licked it."

She frowned. "How?"

"Don't know." He helped her remove the rest of her clothes and after settling her in his sleep-bed, he stripped too. He pulled her into his arms, and his feline stretched sleepily beneath his skin, totally satisfied with the state of affairs.

Gradually she relaxed, her breathing becoming even as she fell asleep. Felix wasn't tired, but he was content to hold her close while his mind raced.

If he ever met the fuckin' general face-to-face, he intended to punch him in the nose and send him sprawling on his smug, arrogant ass.

General Seonaid stood before the floor-to-ceiling windows of his office, his hands clasped behind his back, feet together as he peered out at the view of Dalcon City, the palace, and the mountainous region beyond. But instead of seeing the view and appreciating his accomplishments, the general dwelled on Captain Seonaid.

Captain Seonaid.

He'd like to wring her bloody neck. *Phrull*, he'd do it and enjoy seeing the life seep from her eyes, if her death wouldn't impede his plans.

He wanted to demand a status update from his aide, but he

remained at the window, aware he was starting to raise curiosity. He couldn't afford to let word of his plans get out. Not everyone would appreciate his brilliance.

The general returned to his desk and buzzed his aide. "Refreshments, please. My usual hot lotus juice and something to eat. Anything," he added with a trace of impatience.

"Yes sir."

General Seonaid leaned back in his chair then gave a heavy sigh and pulled up specs on an upcoming mission to Janus, a planet full of militants. He'd concentrate on his mission to build a new base on the planet. No matter the local opinion, the base was necessary, and he intended to see that it succeeded.

His aide tapped on his door and carried in the requested refreshments. "I have news, sir."

The general's stomach lurched, but he kept his expression impassive. "Yes?"

"Captain Seonaid appears to be en route to Dalcon. At least, reconnaissance reported her tracker signal is near the planet."

"Any idea where she came from?" She'd been at a resort on Tiraq. Or at least, his wife had told him their daughter had intended to go there with her guttersnipe friend.

"No, sir. All we know is that her tracker is sending a signal from off planet and the vector indicates a destination of Dalcon."

"Keep me posted."

"Yes, sir."

The general waited until his aide left before he poured himself a glass of hot juice. Satisfaction crawled through him and found an outlet in a rare smile. She'd come around. If she was returning to Dalcon, that meant she was within reach.

He plucked his private com-circle from his pocket and made a call to the head doctor at the military medical center. "Captain Seonaid has returned to Dalcon. Please schedule the surgery for tomorrow."

"Her body will require further preparation before the final transforming nanos are inserted into her system. It will take a solar week while we pump the necessary hormones through her bloodstream."

The general's hand tightened around his com-circle, but he didn't let his impatience bleed into his voice. "Do whatever is necessary. Captain Seonaid will report to the medical facility tomorrow. Expect her." He clicked off the communication and settled back into his chair.

Finally his plan was progressing in the right direction.

Finally, his rebellious daughter was stepping in line with his wishes.

Finally, he'd gain everything he'd worked for, everything he deserved.

CHAPTER ELEVEN

C asey walked through the resort at Felix's side. The funny
blue bird Felix said he was looking after for his brother
waddled after them, trailing like a pet.

She wore a floaty dress, one of her own designs, and early this
morning, she'd decided not to shave her hair again. She was going
to grow it longer. Funny how liberated the decision made her feel.

She'd even allowed herself to believe Felix when he said the
general wouldn't whisk her away to the medical facility.

Felix reached for her hand and laced their fingers. The blue bird
pecked at a patch of light-purple grass and let out a contented
honk. She knew just how the bird felt. With the tracker gone, her
fears had dispersed, the weight of the general's expectation lifting
off her shoulders.

Though, while she felt more relaxed, the analytical part of her
brain—the part that made her a good soldier—wouldn't shut up

with its niggling worries.

It couldn't be this easy. *It couldn't.*

Scarlett came running toward them, perfectly balanced on her new pair of *Elsa* shoes, her long black hair in its normal tight donut bun. "Someone is trying to cut the fence. North quadrant."

They broke into a run, only slowing when they reached the area.

"There he is," Casey said in a low voice.

Not quietly enough, because the man froze and sprang around to face them.

"Laurence," Felix gritted out, surging forward with a furious growl. He grabbed the man by the back of his shirt. "What the fuck do you think you're doing?"

"I'm not doing anything!" Laurence's green gaze skittered, not settling until it found a point over Felix's shoulder. "I found this damage. I'm trying to fix the hole." He wrenched from Felix's grip and put two feet between them, his body language screaming guilt.

Felix let him, but he continued to eye the smaller man as if he were an annoying bug. "You're assigned to work at the shuttle port. The supply vessel is due in soon." Felix crossed his arms. "Why are you out here?"

"It's my break," Laurence said, still avoiding their gazes. He bit down on his bottom lip. "I'm allowed to take a break. You can't make me work all the time."

"Doesn't look like a break to me," Scarlett said. "He's talking too fast and biting his lip. Those are both signs of guilt. What do you think, Casey?"

"He's slumping his shoulders too. That's another sign. Stand straight, man! Have some pride," Casey barked, falling into a military leader role without even thinking about it. "What's in the bucket? Doesn't smell too good."

Felix snarled, obviously adding two plus two and coming up with the same answer as her. "You're feeding them, you bastard! You're doing it on purpose, attracting the zylon, knowing that someone might die from their bite." Felix let out another vicious growl and sprang at Laurence.

The man let out a girlie shriek and tried to run.

Casey slid in front of Felix before he struck the smaller man and took the brunt of Felix's angry charge.

"Oomph!" Casey slammed into Laurence and would have fallen, but Felix held her upright.

"That was silly. A spanking offense," Felix said in a quiet voice meant only for her.

"Promises, promises."

"Playing with fire, sweetheart. I haven't graduated to anything kinky yet, but I'm happy to add variety anytime you say the word."

A shiver sped through Casey, and *she* couldn't meet Felix's gaze either. *Scurvy sky pirates.* The man did things to her insides and made her crave physical touch when she'd never been prey to girlish or romantic notions.

She swallowed upon seeing the promise in his eyes, recalled they had two witnesses, and called on her training again. "Now, wait a minute, Felix. Why don't we give the man a chance to explain?" Casey gave Laurence a friendly smile, intent on playing her part. "What's in the bucket, Laurence?"

"I was feeding the animals."

"Which animals?"

A chitter came from the bushes just outside the fence. A black nose poked out of the pink leaves, pushing out farther to reveal a cute fluffy head and big round eyes.

"Fuck," Felix said.

Casey jabbed Felix with her elbow. "Are you feeding the zylon, Laurence?"

"Yeah." Defiant, he lifted his head—until he caught Felix's furious glare. The color fled his cheeks, and he edged closer to Scarlett.

"Why would you do that?" Casey asked in a pleasant voice.

Low-down dirty scumbag. "The zylon are dangerous. *You* know that. *I* know that. Why would you encourage them to come here, to creep through the holes you've been making in the fence?"

"I didn't— Oh, all right! The Mitchells get *everything*! Everything they do turns to gold. It's not fair! It's *their* fault Lori died. It's their fault I'm on this god-forsaken planet!"

Sniveling of the worst kind. Casey glimpsed the disbelief on Scarlett's face and figured Felix's expression would be a heap worse. Laurence not only expected others to take care of him, but he shifted the blame when things went wrong in his life.

"How old are you?" Casey asked in a soft voice.

"Twenty-eight. What's that got to do with anything?"

"You're old enough to strike out on your own. Why haven't you done that, Laurence? If you don't enjoy living at Middlemarch Resort, then leave. Go to Dalcon. Get a job there or go back to where you came from. No one forced you to move here, to take a job at the resort."

"But they owe me. It's their fault Lori died!"

Scarlett glared and moved into his personal space. "That's *not* true. The virus killed Lori."

Laurence's chin angled up a fraction until Felix growled, and then his shoulders rounded to a slump. It was like watching the beings on Jervois. They had protective shells, and the instant trouble presented, they retracted their heads, retreating into their hard outer skins. Perhaps she should suggest he travel to Jervois.

Laurence coughed to clear his throat, then coughed again. "If...if she hadn't hooked up with Saber, she wouldn't have spent so much time in Middlemarch. She wouldn't have caught the virus."

"Bullshit," Felix said. "Shifter communities in Australia, Canada, USA—they lost people the same as us."

"That's not true. Lori would still be alive—"

"For fuck's sake," Felix muttered. "It's obvious nothing we say will persuade you. But we've seen your complicity with our

149

own eyes. You're letting zylon through the fence. Encouraging the bloody things to come inside the compound by feeding them."

"That's a crime," Scarlett said.

"It's not a *crime*. Besides, I don't force them to bite," Laurence said, this time with a sullen edge to his whine.

"*Scurvy sky pirates*," Casey said. "What is wrong with you? It *is* a crime. A court could charge you with manslaughter if anyone dies."

Laurence made a scoffing sound. "I don't think so."

"Fuck off," Felix snarled and elbowed Scarlett out of his way. "You're not welcome here. Pack your things and *fuck off*."

"You can't do that!" Laurence said.

"Watch me," Felix snapped, and Casey saw the feline in him, saw the elongating of his eyes and the claws extend when he grabbed Laurence by his shirt and shoved him back against the fence. "You don't want to be here. We don't want you. You're lucky I'm not giving you the hiding you deserve." He pushed his face close to Laurence's. "I want to."

"You can't do this!" Laurence's voice took on a bleating tone. *Irritating.*

"When's the next shuttle coming through?" Casey asked. She'd met men like Laurence. Clueless, intent on revenge and stupid with it.

"He can leave on the supply freighter. It's due to arrive later this afternoon," Scarlett said. "I'll arrange his pay and for his stuff to get packed up."

"No. *No!* Please, you can't do this. Shifters don't do well on their own."

"Should have thought of that before," Felix said, and he shoved Laurence toward the resort.

"I hate it here anyway," Laurence spat. "This place is full of sluts with one thing on their minds. It's *disgusting* the way they paw at the staff."

"Yet you were in the office bellyaching about how it wasn't fair you were stuck working at the shuttle port." Felix shoved Laurence farther down the path, and Casey heard Laurence protesting and making excuses until he and Felix rounded the corner in the path and disappeared.

"I never liked him," Scarlett said. "Lori was okay, but there was something off about her too. Not that I'd ever said anything to Saber." She plucked a com-circle out of the pocket of her jacket. "I'll contact the twins and get them to fix the fence. Hopefully it's for the last time, now that we've caught the culprit in the act." She spoke with one of her brothers and disconnected. "Will you be okay here until Sly and Joe arrive?"

"No prob. He didn't finish cutting the fence anyway."

Left alone, she turned her attention to the fence. Bluebird honked and appeared behind her, waddling here and there to peck at plants. On the other side of the fence, two zylon sniffed the bushes. Hard to think their bite was so dangerous. They looked like harmless fluffy balls.

Felix appeared with a bag of tools slung over his shoulder.

"That was quick."

"Joe and Sly escorted Laurence back to his quarters to pack. They'll put him on the freighter."

"He was shortchanged in the brain department."

Felix snorted. "You're not wrong there. Hold this part of the fence for me, will ya?"

Casey held the bit Felix indicated. "So you've caught the phantom fence cutter."

Felix let out a laugh. "At least that will be one less thing for Saber to worry about when he returns. Eva is coming back with him."

"Eva? But what about her restaurants?"

"Saber will talk her around." Felix used the auto-bang to fasten the last staple. "I'm not intending to let you go either, Casey."

She frowned at him and started to speak.

He clapped his hand over her mouth and kissed the tip of her nose. "Don't argue because you won't win."

The second he removed his hand, she spoke. He had to listen. "The general isn't stupid. He'll figure it out eventually and come looking for me."

"If he comes looking, you'll tell him to take a running jump," Felix said. "You'll tell him you intend to stay here with me. You'll tell him you love me."

"I don't love you. We haven't known each other long enough."

Her blunt words seemed to hang in the air between them, and she wished she could snatch them back. They mightn't have known each other for long, but she cared for him. The thought of leaving and never seeing him again ate at her like a flesh-eating bug.

"Maybe you don't yet, but you will," Felix said with smug confidence. "You won't be able to resist me for much longer." He reached for her hand and towed her back toward the main resort buildings.

"But I'm a soldier." She wasn't qualified to do anything else, a fact the general had pointed out to her.

"No, you're a fashion designer and a boutique manager," Felix countered. "You're my lover and my mate. You're Eva's friend."

Casey sighed at his descriptions, a large part of her wanting to believe his words, but a tiny voice at the back of her mind didn't think the general would give up as easily as they expected.

"Don't," Felix said. "Don't think of him. Don't give him the power to hurt you."

"How am I meant to forget? I've spent most of my life trying to please the general, most of my career trying to gain his approval. It's difficult to switch off the need for praise."

"Hell, Casey." Felix stopped walking and cupped her face in his hands. "I intend to fill your days with work and your nights with loving. I intend to keep you so busy that you won't have time to brood about the general and the things missing in your relationship with your parents."

Hard to put her faith in his words. He didn't know the general, didn't understand the depths he'd go to get his own way. She'd seen him in action. "Aunt Elsa and your mother have everything under control. There's not much for me to do with the boutique."

"So get out your design tablet and get designing. Start working on designs so the boutique has products to sell."

He made it sound so simple. "But what if the general is right, and I have no talent for anything apart from the military?"

"Say that again, and I will spank you."

Casey closed her eyes and fought to quell the stirrings of panic. Her fears for their safety, her aunt's safety. Hell, *her* safety.

"Start with a project you can sew quickly and show the women how to make the garment. Start small and get your confidence going. Casey, the few women here need this as much as you do. Everything is different and new to us all. We're struggling to make a new life for ourselves. We've lost family and friends to the virus. How are any of us different from you?"

Casey winced. "You're right. I rarely hide from things that scare me."

"Everyone has an off day, sweetheart. Don't you think I'm worried about failing? Saber does everything well. Our people count on him, and sometimes, I feel as if I'm floundering and lost in the mighty shadow he casts. Yet, he left me in charge and trusted me to take care of things. It's made me realize I don't *have* to stand in his shadow. What I need to do—what we both need to do—is step forward with confidence and let ourselves make mistakes. As long as we learn from them, it doesn't matter. What do you say, sweetheart?" He offered his hand. "Walk at my side. Share this adventure with me."

Casey gave a small laugh. "Okay. Yes."

He tugged her down the path toward his suite. "Are you sure you don't love me?"

"Maybe just a little," she said.

"Glad to hear it. Now what are you going to make first for the boutique? What materials do we need to order?"

"Aunt Elsa brought quite a few lengths of fabric with her. Enough for me to start. I'll speak with her and Anna now."

"Good girl," Felix said and she basked in the warmth of his approval. The sensation radiated through her chest and heated her up in a good way. A smile pushed her lips into a curve before she knew it was happening, and even better, he grinned back at her and squeezed her hand.

Happiness, she thought. Real happiness.

At his suite, they parted. Felix went to oversee the arrival of the supplies and Laurence's departure while she searched out Aunt Elsa and Anna.

"What happened to the fabrics you brought for me?" she asked.

Her aunt beamed. "Have you decided to stay?"

Casey gave a cautious nod and liked how felt too. "Yes." Her reply, a little loud, made her aunt chuckle.

"A new adventure for both of us," her aunt said and gave Casey a hug.

"I'm so pleased you're staying," Anna said.

"Felix said I should make something to sell at the boutique, something I can teach the ladies to make. I thought that we could start with a plain sleeveless base, like a slip, but in a lovely fabric that isn't see-through. Then make a transparent top or jacket to go over the top. The jacket or tops could be in lacy fabrics or patterned gauze, and if a lady purchased several different tops, it would appear as if she had more than one outfit, even though the base would be the same.

"I can design a resort label too. I was thinking the head of a black cat with the words Middlemarch Resort." Casey finished talking and clenched her fingers while waiting for the older ladies to comment. She wiped the palms of her hands on her dress and worked hard to remain in one spot. *Scurvy sky pirates.* This was worse than handing out orders to her men.

"Oh," Anna said. "That is brilliant. There are several ladies I can think of who can sew and would love to be part of this. What a wonderful idea to include them."

"It was Felix's idea," Casey said. "The outfits—should I make the ones I have in mind to show you?"

"Yes, please."

"All the fabric is in my room," Aunt Elsa said. "Would you like me to design the label for you?"

"You both like my idea?"

"It's perfect, dear," Anna said, beaming. "I thought I'd said that."

"I agree," Aunt Elsa said. "The foundation garment could be in any color, but I think you should make the first one a pale pink to go with the local scenery. There is nothing like this on Dalcon, at least not near the city, and that could be the garment that the guests associate with the resort when they return from their vacation."

"Do you think Scarlett would be my model?"

"Yes," Anna said without hesitation. "Even if I have to drag her away from her computers. Not that I think she'll put up much of a fight. In fact, I'll see her in person, so she can't dodge my call." Anna scurried away, leaving Casey alone with her aunt.

"I'm so pleased," Aunt Elsa said. "This will be a fresh start for both of us. I have to admit I'm glad to leave the bustle of Dalcon. The city is so big now and parts have become dangerous. The resort is peaceful and the beach is gorgeous. The sea air has helped my chest."

Casey frowned. "Why did you stay on Dalcon for so long?"

"Because I wanted to spend time with *you*, Casey. Now, let's get that fabric and see what we've got. I am positive we have pink, but I'm not sure if the fabric will be what you have in mind. And, of course, pink won't suit everyone. Some of the other species will prefer stronger colors."

Casey followed her aunt to her room and spent the rest of the afternoon discussing fabrics, cutting and stitching. Anna arrived with Scarlett, and soon she had the garment fitted and pinned.

"Ouch," Scarlett muttered.

"Sorry," Casey said. "I told you to stand still."

"I need to breathe," Scarlett said, but the twinkle in her green eyes told Casey the younger woman was teasing.

The rest of the day flew by. Felix arrived, and the twins popped in to report on their progress.

"We planted the vines," Joe said.

"The grapevines?" Anna asked with a touch of surprise.

"We checked the soil, did some tests, and Felix agreed. It was time, Ma," Sly said.

"But Saber—"

"He put me in charge, Ma," Felix said. "We're all experienced in winegrowing and production. If Saber has a problem, he'll let us know, but the conditions are perfect, and we've taken precautions to make sure none of the local fauna can attack or eat the plants—at least until they become established. Saber has enough to worry about, and we're all trying to lighten his load."

Anna's face softened. "I'm sorry, Felix. You're right. Saber needs some time for himself. I know all my sons are capable."

She patted his shoulder, and Casey sensed the tension in Felix drain away.

In his own way, he was struggling to find his place as much as her.

"Alone at last," Felix whispered. "I didn't think I was ever going to pry you loose from my sister and mother and your aunt."

Casey chuckled. "Telling them you wanted some alone time did the trick. Your mother and my aunt practically pushed us out the door." She touched her fingertips to her cheeks. "I'm still embarrassed."

"It looks good on you," he said and pressed his palm to the doorplate to let them into his suite.

He hustled her inside and closed the door after them, engaging the locks. His eyes were bright green when he turned her to face him, and a lazy smile curved his lips, making her heart beat a little faster.

"Strip," he said. "It's time for that spanking I owe you, sweetheart."

"No," she said, backing away and laughing at the same time.

"Yes." Felix prowled closer. "You might laugh, but I'm serious. I don't like you putting yourself in danger. You're precious to me."

Her heart went pitter-patter at his words because she had no doubts—he meant what he said. "I'm not a fan of danger myself."

"Good, then you'll understand why I have to do this." He pounced without warning, and before she knew it, she was sprawled facedown over his knee.

"Felix!" She scissored her legs, kicking and wriggling to get free, but he held her easily. She let the tension seep from her body, waited for the instant when he'd relax too—and then kicked hard again.

"All your wriggling is turning me on, sweetheart."

"Make me grumpy enough, and I might bite."

"Might," he said. "I don't think you'd hurt me on purpose, just as I'd never hurt you."

"I'm a soldier. I know lots of ways to injure you."

"I'm a shifter. I can tear you limb from limb and then eat the evidence."

"Checkmate," she said drily. "You win."

Felix hauled her up to face him. "It's not a case of winning. You *can* hurt me, you know. I feel a bond with you. I ache for you when we're not together. If you were to reject me and refuse to stay with me, that would hurt. It would hurt far worse than physical pain."

Casey stared, taking in his strong features, his beautiful green eyes, and his serious expression. "You mean it."

"This mark." He traced the curious tattoo that had appeared after he bit her, and a bolt of pleasure ripped through her. He continued despite her gasp. "This mark ties me to you. I don't know how it works, but this was how shifters claimed their mates centuries ago. If you were a shifter, you'd bite me in return. This mark is as solid as marriage vows."

"In your eyes we're married?"

"Yes." His gaze never left hers. "You're mine, and I belong to you. Only death will break the bond."

She shivered, and this time, there was no pleasure in the sensation. The tiny hairs on the back of her neck rose, and a chill prickled her skin.

The general would kill Felix and any of his family members who got in his way. She didn't believe he'd give up. Not really. No matter what she tried to tell herself—

She forcibly shoved the general from her thoughts. He dwelled there way too often, much like a malignant growth. She couldn't give him the power and refused to when she could spend the time more enjoyably with Felix.

"I don't like to think of you dying." *Not much of a shove.* "Tell me more about shifters."

"A lot of the old ways, the old instincts, have been lost since we integrated with the humans on Earth and lived in secret. The mating mark thing—that hasn't happened for centuries. And Ma doesn't remember reading anything about the shape of the mark. She's busy researching in the family diaries and papers."

"Your mother keeps a diary?"

"Yes. She likes to record things. Genealogy is one of her

hobbies." His eyes gleamed extra bright. "What about children? Would you like to have children one day?"

Casey felt her mouth drop open, and Felix chuckled.

"I can see you've never thought on the subject."

"I haven't, not seriously. I'm a career soldier. Besides, I didn't think I'd make a good parent, and I've never had a long relationship with a man. I suppose I could have chosen a child from the baby farms. Lots of planets have them."

"We are *not* doing that," Felix said. "They really have farms for babies?"

"Fertility is a problem for the species on some planets. It's the only way some people can have children."

"But what about the parents? The women who carry the children? What do they think about giving their offspring away?"

Casey laughed. "No, they make the babies in test tubes. In a clinical factory. It's very common and—"

"We're making our children the normal way," Felix said in a firm tone. "I want to see you swell with my children."

"Children?" Casey squeaked. "They come in a litter?"

Felix barked out a laugh. "Twins are common, although in our family there only ever seems to be one set in each union. My mother had Sly and Joe. Mostly, the twins are the same sex and identical. Laurence and his sister Lori were unusual."

"Interesting," Casey said.

"So you'll think about having children in the future?" Felix asked. "I'd like that very much."

"And if I can't have children?"

"Then we will visit the baby farm—if that's what you want. Children are an extra bonus for me. You're the important part of this relationship."

"You say the most amazing things." She kissed the tip of his nose.

"So you like me a little bit?"

"I like you a lot," Casey said. An understatement. The man had wriggled under her skin like a persistent itch, and now she found she didn't want to dislodge him. She liked the future he painted, was even starting to dream of making it a reality.

"Glad to hear it," he said.

He grasped her waist and laid her over his knee again. Before she gathered her wits enough to protest, his hand smacked down on her rump.

"*Ow.*"

"Because you've been so sweet, I'm going to limit the number to five," he said.

Seconds later, another blow landed. The scanty covering of her dress and panties didn't protect her one bit, and the sting rushed along her nerve pathways. She'd scarcely processed the pain and had time to protest before another two landed in quick succession.

"One more," he said.

"You're mean, and I take it back." She tried to wriggle free. "I don't like you anymore."

"Two more it is."

Smack. Smack.

He lifted her off his knee and steadied her on her feet.

She backed up several steps and eyed him, saw the brief flash of satisfaction, then the wariness that shone in his eyes. "That was plain mean. I'm a soldier, and I'm used to putting myself in dangerous situations. You can't smack me for doing my job."

"Just did."

There was that arrogance again. She sniffed and stuck her nose in the air, but a tiny part of her wanted to laugh too. The man was impossible, but it was hard not to like him. "I was doing my job," she repeated.

It was that or breaking out the humor, and she didn't want to fold so soon, not when her backside still smarted.

"Maybe so, but there's a difference between dangerous and reckless. I aged, Casey. When I had to let you go off with those natives, I worried. Why the hell do you think we arrived at the village so quickly? I pushed and pushed hard to get there."

"Aw, Felix." The tone of his voice, his agitation and obvious anguish, smoothed away her lingering pique. "How about if I promise to think harder before throwing myself into a dangerous situation again?"

"You're not a soldier now," he reminded her. "You're my mate and the resort's exclusive designer. You won't face danger again unless you prick your finger with the sewing machine."

"The new ones stop the second they come into contact with skin."

He muttered something under his breath. "Don't be obtuse. You know what I mean." He prowled toward her and looked mighty fine doing it. Mesmerized, she stared and then it was too late. He scooped her up and tossed her on the sleep-bed, caging her between his hard body and the mattress. His mouth crushed down on hers, his fingers sliding beneath the neckline of her dress to cup her breast.

"My backside is sore," she said when he lifted his head. "You need to rub it."

"With pleasure. Let's get you out of these clothes."

"You first."

"Your ass can't be hurtin' too bad then. Maybe I should've given you more strokes."

Casey sniffed and battled her urge to laugh again. "Did I tell you I have training in hand-to-hand combat? I could do a lot of damage to your pretty person. As long as you didn't go hairy, I'd win."

He flashed a grin. "You looking for a sparring partner? Could be fun. A little sparring, then some hot jungle sex."

"I've had sex in the hot jungle. There are red bugs, and they bite."

Felix unbuttoned his shirt and let it fall to the ground. He made quick work of the rest of his clothes and stood before her naked and unashamed. "Just hot sex will do nicely then. Strip for me." He sprawled on the sleep-bed, his avid gaze hot and transmitting a silent dare.

This time she let her grin run free. She swayed and lifted her arms. A sensual hip roll snagged his gaze, and she laughed, a joyful sound. "You're easy, Felix."

"I am where you're concerned."

She unfastened her dress and let it slide to the ground and land in a pool of fabric. Striking a pose, she blew him a kiss. "What do you think?"

The apricot-colored lingerie flattered her curves, and when Felix rose to a sitting position, she knew she had him.

"God, Casey. You're beautiful." He held out his hand, and she went to him. "Let me undress you."

"Not yet. I want to explore *you* for a change." She placed her hand in the middle of his chest and pushed. He let her, and the protection around her heart cracked a little more. This man—he undid her. So different from all the other men she knew.

Casey straddled his hips. His cock was full and jutted out, but she ignored his erection to explore his shoulders and chest. She licked the base of his neck, and remembering how it felt when he kissed and nipped her there, she scraped her teeth over the spot.

He let out a harsh moan, his hands rising to grip her shoulders and hold her in place. "Bite harder."

"But I'll hurt you."

"Don't care."

She bit down, and a shudder went through his big body. She licked the spot and went on with her explorations, trailing her fingers down his biceps. So much male bounty to explore. She'd never taken the time before, had never wanted to play. She kissed, took the odd nip, and teased him with her touches.

"Casey," he groaned in protest.

He trembled, and she wondered if he'd take over, but he

remained in place and let her have her way. She moved down his body, gripped his cock, and stroked down his length. A bead of liquid formed on the tip. Curious, she dipped her head to taste him. Slightly salty. A little musky.

"More," he said. "Please."

At that moment, she knew she'd do anything for this man. He was special, so special. She took him into her mouth and licked, sucked, tested him for reactions.

His hands went to her head, cupping her skull and holding her in place. She breathed in his scent, reveled in the power she had over him, the way her touches made his big body quiver with need.

"Damn, that feels good," he said. "I'd like more, but I want to come with you tonight. I want to slide into your sexy body and feel your tight sex caress my shaft. I want to push you hard and fast and drive into your body. Then, once you're trembling beneath me, I'll stroke your mark. Make you come so violently your body shudders with the pleasure."

Casey pulled off his cock with a popping sound. "Sounds good. What's stopping you?"

Primitive hunger etched his face. Raw male desire focused on her. "Get on your back and spread your legs for me," he said.

After holding his gaze for a fraction longer, she quickly removed her lingerie and followed his instructions.

"You are so beautiful." He ran his hand over her hip and skimmed her inner thigh. He dipped his head and ran his tongue down her folds. He rubbed her clit, the roughness of his tongue sending clawing hunger through her. He'd barely touched her, yet she wanted him so badly. The swirl of his warm, wet tongue sent her nerve endings snapping. One finger slipped inside her and stroked while his tongue teased the straining bundle of nerves. A light flicker of a touch. Casey groaned, her hips lifting toward his mouth.

"Please, Felix." An orgasm built, layer upon layer, with each touch, each lick, each enticing kiss. Her pulse skittered as sensation flared and burned. Her hips jerked and bucked beneath the pleasurable assault. Another finger filled her and stroked her inner walls. Combined with the lash of his tongue, it was too much, and the sensations collided in a storm of ecstasy.

While tiny spasms still quivered through her, Felix rose and pushed inside her to the hilt. A moan rolled up her throat and emerged as he pulled back and sank deep again. Flesh slapped against flesh. His teeth scored the tender skin of her mark, and pleasure coursed through her body. He flailed it with his tongue, and she sucked in a greedy breath at the quick punch of heat. A second climax broke over her, not as powerful as the first but still breath-stealing.

As soon as she started coming, he buried himself in her and came with hot groans. He curled over her, surrounding her with his heat and giving her some of his weight. He kissed the side of the neck and lifted up to smile at her. "That was fun."

She stared at him, her pulse racing like a wild creature intent on capturing its quarry. She wanted him to say more—say he loved her. If she was honest, that was where her feelings were headed. She grinned back. "Most of it was fun."

"Just keep sensible decisions in mind, sweetheart."

"Are you threatening me?"

"Nope," he said. "I'm promising." Then he kissed her again, and that was the last time they spoke for a long time.

CHAPTER TWELVE

The general stood at his office window and peered out at the lights of the cityscape. He clasped his hands behind his back and stood military-straight.

A tap sounded on his door. "General."

"I told you not to interrupt me."

"Sir, I have located Captain Seonaid."

Elation filled the general, and he turned to face his aide. "Where?"

"She's still at Middlemarch Resort, sir."

"But her tracker... How is this possible? I thought you located the tracker on Dalcon before it moved away toward an unknown destination?"

"Yes, sir, but my contact says she's at the resort."

The general frowned, envisioning potential problems if he sent a team to extract her and she wasn't there. "This contact is reliable?"

"He's an ex-employee of the resort. I saw him in person and showed him a photo of Captain Seonaid. He confirmed she is staying at the resort."

"Good. Good. That is excellent." He turned back to stare at the lights of the city. Beyond the cityscape, the darkness of the mountainous region loomed, inhospitable and full of danger. The unknown...much like the surprisingly unpredictable actions of Captain Seonaid.

What to do?

He tapped his fingers against his thigh, sucked in a deep breath, and let it ease back out. "Order the black ops team to move. We'll extract her from the resort and take her to the medical facility. Tell them to move tomorrow night."

"Sir, do you—"

"Tomorrow night. And I expect to be kept up to date on the progress of the extraction."

"We're going for a walk," Felix said to his mother and siblings.

"You just want to kiss and grope Casey in the dark," Scarlett said and waggled her eyebrows at Casey. "I bet he's icky at kissing. Actually, I don't want to think about my brother kissing. *Blah.*"

"Change the subject then," Felix said and pinched Scarlett's arm. "Casey doesn't have any complaints."

Scarlett wrinkled her nose and danced out of reach. "It's not fair that you can talk about sex when there's no hope of anyone for me."

"You're too young," Anna said.

"Ma, I'm twenty," Scarlett said. "You married Dad when you were eighteen."

Casey grinned at Scarlett's plaintive tone even as she enjoyed the dynamics between the different family members.

"I don't believe I mentioned sex," Felix said. "I asked Casey to take a walk with me."

"The implication was there," Sly said, taking Scarlett's side.

"I have to vote with Sly and Scarlett," Joe agreed.

"We're not appreciated here," Felix said and held out his hand to her, one green eye closing in a wink. "Let's make out in the dark."

"Anytime," she said.

She was laughing as she laced her fingers with Felix's and followed him out of his mother's suite. She liked the Mitchell family and enjoyed their teasing and the way they made her feel part of the group.

Aunt Elsa liked them a lot, and her last words before she left to settle her business affairs for her move to the resort were, "He's a keeper. I'm so happy for you."

As for her own feelings, Felix had worn away her reservations, and it was easy to see how her life would go with him. They'd be happy. Oh, they might disagree sometimes, but she considered that healthy, and she thought with a delicate shiver, making up would be a pleasure. "Are we really going for a walk?"

"I thought we'd check the fence, just in case there's more than one person trying to hack holes in the perimeter. I also want to see if there are any zylon on the other side of the fence. The population is less than it used to be, but we need to keep it that way for the safety of the guests."

"The resort looks pretty at night with all the colored lights. How are the new guests shaping up? Are they behaving?"

"Everything seems to be going well." Felix steered her into the shadows and drew her close. "I don't want to talk about guests."

His kiss was easy, and the tenderness with which he kissed started a slow burn in her pussy.

"Hmm, more," she whispered when he lifted his head. She wrapped her hands around his neck and drew him down for another seductive taste.

He brushed her cheek in the casual yet affectionate way she'd come to enjoy. "This isn't getting the fence checked."

"I thought the silent alarm was enough?"

"I didn't say anything to the others, but I got the sense someone was watching earlier in the day."

"From the other side of the fence? Not the chief or one of his men?" He was confiding in her, sharing his concerns, and it knocked yet another flimsy barrier away.

Scurvy sky pirates, where was her mind?

The truth was, Felix, aided by his boisterous siblings, had charmed her and shown more love than she'd ever received. Heck, all of them had seduced her to their way of thinking what family should be.

"I think they would've come to say hello since they know me now."

"I agree. Was anyone working outside the fence today? Could Laurence have returned?" she asked.

"Laurence has no guts. He'll be on Dalcon, where he was sent, having his normal pity party."

"Harsh."

"But true. The man has always been a sniveling idiot."

They walked hand in hand, the gravel path crunching beneath their boots. Somewhere, a night bird cried out, and invisible insects hummed in chorus.

As they rounded a corner in the path, the night noises Casey had become used to suddenly ceased.

"You're right," she murmured, putting her mouth next to his ear so the sound didn't carry. "Someone or something is out there." She kept ambling, every sense hyper-alert.

"I can't scent anything," Felix said after a while.

They followed the circular path until they arrived back at the main part of the resort. Feminine laughter floated on the air, the occasional male voice.

"Business as usual here," he said.

A burst of fear struck her right in the heart. "What if the general has sent a squad for me?"

"That would be illegal. You're not military any longer, and your tracker is gone." Felix turned her to face him. "If that happens, we'll deal with it. You're not going anywhere. You're my captive."

Casey let out a scoffing sound. "It's a hard life but someone has to do it."

"Not someone. You."

"Me," she agreed and realized she'd never hesitated.

As they neared Felix's suite, a frisson of awareness hit her. She kept walking but felt the weight of a stare pressing against her flesh. She shuddered and prayed it was an overactive imagination. But she didn't think so.

Only when they were inside their suite did she start to relax.

"I think you're right," she said. "Something was out there."

"You felt it too," Felix said.

She nodded. "What are we going to do?"

"Nothing right now. The alarm is on and functioning. While you're getting ready for bed, I'll let my brothers know something is off. Tomorrow we'll check it out."

"In cat form?"

"Yes."

Casey twisted his plan in her mind and finally nodded. "That's a good idea."

"If there's anything untoward, we'll know and can make plans."

Casey wrapped her arms around him and gave him a quick kiss. "You're good at this stuff."

"Thanks, sweetheart."

The fence alarm woke them in the early hours of the morning.

Casey dressed and snatched up her weapon. "I'm coming with you."

Felix gave a curt nod. "Stay close."

They slipped from their suite, Felix still in human form. His brothers had already shifted and stalked along the path in front of them.

A single form, dressed in black, flitted across the path. Felix's brothers prowled through the shadows after him. The gravel crunched up ahead.

"Shoot to wound," Felix whispered against her ear. "We want to question them."

Casey kept close to Felix and tried to emulate his silent footfalls. Not easy on a gravel path.

A shout rang out to their right. A feral snarl.

"Retreat," a low voice said. "I repeat. Retreat!"

A familiar voice.

Casey tugged on Felix's arm. "That's one of my brothers."

Another menacing snarl carried on the air. A panicked scream. The sound of running feet.

Casey ran behind Felix, no longer worried about noise.

"Here's the hole," Felix said in a grim voice. "They've gotten away."

A fierce growl sounded behind them, and Casey turned. One of Felix's brothers dragged an unconscious man by the arm. Two other cats trotted behind. The big cat dropped the man on the path under a light.

Felix kneeled and pulled off the man's headwear. "Recognize him?"

"My brother William," Casey said in a grim tone. She stalked over and poked him with her boot. "You can wake up now, Lieutenant."

"Captain," he murmured, warily eyeing the silent cats that

surrounded him.

"*Casey*," she said in a firm voice. "What the *phrull* are you doing here?"

"The general wants to see you," William said.

"He couldn't use a communicator like a normal person?" Felix demanded.

"Who are *you*?"

"Casey's fiancé."

Surprise suffused Casey. They hadn't discussed marriage yet, but it warmed her through to learn Felix's intentions. Sometimes she got the feeling he was moving slower than he preferred, but he was proceeding with caution so he didn't scare her away.

"The general won't give up," William said.

Felix grabbed William and hoisted him to his feet with effortless strength. Casey almost laughed at the shocked expression on her brother's face.

"I want you to give the general a message. You tell him Casey is no longer in the military. You tell the asshole from me that Casey has *no intention* of entering the medical facility to undergo the procedure to change sexes. And finally, you tell him if he doesn't back the hell off and leave Casey alone, we'll break the story in a public manner that will embarrass the general and humiliate the military. Have you got all that?"

"He wants you to become a man?" William asked, his horrified gaze on Casey.

"Yes." A tight knot formed in her throat, and she couldn't force out another word. Felix took one look and went to her, slipping his arm around her shoulders.

"Why would he do that?" William demanded.

"You'll have to ask *him* that," Felix snapped. "You make sure he realizes Casey is out of his reach. Got it?"

William nodded. "I understand. You can call off your trained cats now."

Felix snapped his fingers, and his brothers backed away and went to sit beside Casey.

William brushed himself off and limped toward the hole in the fence.

Typical, Casey thought.

But upon reaching the fence, William turned, his gaze going straight to Casey. "I'm sorry. I didn't know you were the one we were meant to extract. I was assigned to hold our perimeter, someone else was tasked to obtain the target. The general... I'm sorry," he repeated, then he was gone, his black uniform blending with the darkness.

"Where is she?" the general barked into his communicator. "I want to see her before she goes into the medical facility. Have Captain Seonaid escorted to my office."

"Ah, sir," the soldier in charge of extraction said. "We don't have Captain Seonaid. The mission failed."

"What?" The general's bark took on an edge of bite. A snarly quality that warned his subordinates to tread warily. "You're telling me our best black ops team failed a mission?"

"They seemed to know we were coming, sir. They were prepared, and they have large black cats patrolling the resort."

"Did you have weapons?" The vein at his temple started pulsing, and the general pressed a finger against it. *Stupid imbeciles.* How could they mess up such a simple mission? One puny woman to extract and they messed it up.

"The cats attacked Lieutenant Seonaid, sir. He barely managed to escape."

"Let me talk to him." Gods, his one weak daughter constantly outshone her brothers.

"He's not here, sir. He's having his arm treated."

The vein pulsed a fraction harder and for a moment, the general thought it might pop. His brain felt the same way—too big for his skull to contain. It pulsed and ached. "Have the lieutenant contact me on my direct personal line. Immediately," he added, lest the squadron leader have any doubts as to the depths of their failure. He cut communications and leaped from his chair, the urge for movement a compulsion.

He paced back and forth.

He'd get his way. There was a reason he'd risen to the rank of general. Because he was smart. He saw the overall picture rather than single components. He deserved this promotion, and if his stupid bitch of a daughter *phrulled* it up for him, heads would roll. He'd stomp her into the ground, and then he'd obliterate the people who were sheltering her. Scaly *phrull*-ups!

A tap sounded on his door, halting him midstride. "Enter," he snapped.

"Sir, I thought you should read this." His aide cautiously extended his arm, the paper he held rustling when he failed to control his nerves.

Idiots. He was surrounded by namby-pamby *phrullin'* idiots.

He snatched the paper, scanned the headlines, and tossed it away in disgust. "It's a gossip sheet. Why should I waste time looking at this rubbish?"

His aide gave an audible swallow and looked as if he might faint. He swallowed again. "There's a paragraph in the gossip pages," he said.

"Spit it out, man."

"It's about your daughter," the aide said in a rush. Now he seemed desperate to get his words out.

And run, no doubt.

"Give me a précis."

His aide darted a glance in his direction. His face was pale and beads of sweat had formed on his pasty forehead. "An anonymous source is quoted as saying that you're forcing your daughter to have a sex change with nanotechnology. They're saying you've never acted like a father to her and that you have no use for the female sex."

Holy phrullin' gods.

A sliver of panic struck him in the middle of the chest. He lifted his hand, rubbed the spot and continued to glare at his aide. "What else?"

"That's all, sir, but other media outlets are picking up the story. I've had two reporters contact this office for a statement."

"If anyone else contacts you, tell them this is a mess of vicious lies, and you have no idea where the story has come from. You tell them this office denies the allegations, and we will stringently defend our honor. Do you understand?"

His aide gulped. "Yes, sir." He backed from the office, and he could feel the man's relief as the distance between them lengthened. The door shut behind him with an audible click.

Where the *phrull* was his son? He needed a situation report stat before this entire *phrulled-up* situation spiraled out of his control.

He could imagine his competition, smirking and rubbing his hands together. *Phrull*, he wouldn't put it past the man to spread the rumors.

These people lacked vision. Females shouldn't be in the military. They weren't mentally strong enough. Any fool could see that. The idiots who kept recommending his daughter for promotion were morons. He'd quashed the last two reports citing actions above and beyond the call of duty. She didn't deserve a promotion. She was a *female.*

Inferior, and good for one thing.

He was doing his best for her, trying to improve her and look what thanks he received. She was attempting to drag his name through the gutters of Dalcon and beyond. He'd sacrificed too much and worked too hard to let her win this battle. His father, his grandfather, and various male relations had all excelled, taking after their proud forebears with their military prowess. He could do nothing less than follow in their illustrious footsteps and set a precedent for his sons.

His *three* sons.

This promotion belonged to him, and nothing, *nothing* would get in his way.

His large-screen communicator buzzed. He snatched the control off the corner of his desk. "General Seonaid."

"General. Lieutenant Seonaid reporting." His son stood at attention, his brown eyes staring straight ahead, his expression full of the necessary respect. His uniform fit him like a glove—the perfect physical specimen. It was a pity his sister had received the larger portion of brains.

"What happened? Why don't you have Captain Seonaid?" he demanded, getting straight to the point.

"They were ready for us. They knew we were coming."

The general felt the vein at his temple pulse again, the urge to pace to dispel the tension residing in the pit of his gut. He forced it back, not wanting his son to witness his unease. "How did they know? You're black ops. You go in prepared. Didn't you reconnoiter beforehand?"

"The resort has a fence around it, but we saw nothing that would make us expect the ability to repel an attack."

Gods, phrullin' excuses. "I want Captain Seonaid."

A brief hesitation. "Sir, she told me you intend to force her to endure nanotechnology."

"I gave orders to have her sent to the medical facility. I didn't tell you to interrogate her for the *reason* behind the order." He wanted to rub his temple, to coax the pulsing vein to remain still, but instead, he remained at attention, his features impassive. "You will go back tonight. You *will* deliver Captain Seonaid to the medical facility and contact me the minute you arrive. Keep her under control until I arrive to speak with her."

Lieutenant Seonaid lifted his chin, the only indication he didn't agree with the order. "Casey isn't a member of military personnel any longer. She completed her term of service and resigned. We have no right to detain her. *Sir.*"

Huh. His son had found his balls. "Do not question my orders!" he thundered. The lieutenant flinched, and momentary satisfaction flooded the general. "Is that clear?"

"Yes, sir."

"I expect her to be at the facility tomorrow morning. Without fail." He clicked off and gave in to the urge to pace. The general stalked to and fro in front of his window, the view of the city not as comforting as normal.

Perhaps he should work this from another angle. His daughter cared for her aunt and had spent most of her leave with his wife's sister. If he threatened Elsa, his daughter would step in line with his wishes.

He found himself smiling and the expression felt foreign on his lips. But he felt a sense of triumph returning and the promise of success.

His daughter would crack like a tree during a Worra sandstorm if he got his hands on her aunt.

The general buzzed his aide and issued additional orders. His smile widened, and he moved to stand at his window. Somewhere down in the city, Elsa Torrens was going about her business. All these years, she'd interfered in his life. It would be a pleasure—*his* pleasure—to knock her off her stride.

No sooner had Casey closed her eyes the very next evening than the alarm went off, dragging her from sleep.

"If that's those black ops guys again, I'm gonna be pissed," Felix muttered. "I'll bite them."

"If it's black ops, I'll be doing some biting of my own." Casey scrambled into her clothes and grabbed her weapon. She hesitated before rifling through her gear for a knife, which she tucked in her boot.

Before she reached the door, it flew open, and two strangers burst inside the suite.

"Hands where I can see them," one ordered.

The other—her oldest brother—merely pointed his weapon in a watchful manner.

"Drop your weapons on the floor," the first one said and glanced at Felix. "You too."

Felix lifted his hands to show they were empty. "No weapons."

He moved to the right, and the two soldiers tracked him with their eyes and weapons. She knew what Felix was doing—taking their focus away from the entrance.

The ex-soldier in her wanted to chew their butts for not covering their asses. Her brother should know better, but she wasn't about to warn them of the impending ambush.

"I'm not military any longer." Casey's voice was calm, belying none of her nervousness. "If you kidnap me from the resort, I've left full details with my friends. They will publicize the story. While I might lose my identity, the general will lose his too—and his *job*—and you'll all be dragged down with him. Think of that before you try to force me to leave against my will."

"I don't believe the things you told William," her brother Jonathan said. "You're lying."

"It's easy enough to prove," Felix said. "Check with the medical facility. See what they say."

"No one asked you. Who the *phrull* are you anyway?"

"I'm Casey's husband," Felix said. "We got married today. And

I'll be one of the people who create a huge fuss if something happens to Casey."

Casey grinned. "Thanks, husband." She waved her hand in the air, the light catching the golden glint of her wedding ring.

From the corner of her eye, she caught a flash of black. The cavalry had arrived.

Two black leopards stalked into position. They glanced at each other in a quick form of communication then pounced, knocking the two men off their feet.

Jonathan cursed, attempted to get up, but one of the twins snarled, snapped his teeth close to Jonathan's face. Her brother froze.

A third black cat trotted up to Felix and gave a grunt. He settled on his haunches beside Casey, and she reached out to run her hand over the cat's head. He purred, and Jonathan stared at her in disbelief.

"You're married to him?" he asked finally.

"Yes."

Felix reached out to draw her against his side and away from his brother. He let one hand settle on her belly. "And she's pregnant. She doesn't consent to any medical tests that might harm our baby."

Ooh, good one, Casey thought. Jonathan knew what went on at the medical facility. He had to. There were rumors...rumors about soldiers who went in and never came out.

"He's *really* forcing you to undergo nanotechnology? And you didn't consent?" Jonathan asked, a strange expression taking residence on his face.

"No. I didn't resign of my own volition, either. The general forced me to," Casey said. "He arranged everything and told me how it would be without giving me a choice."

"Why didn't you say something? Tell me?" Jonathan asked.

Casey snorted. "The general doesn't encourage close family

relations. You don't believe me now, and you wouldn't have believed me earlier. What was I meant to do?"

"I'm going to stand up," Jonathan said. "I'm not going to do anything stupid."

The cat sitting beside him shifted enough to let him move, and he stood carefully. "I want to show you something." He pulled back his sleeve. "I still have a difficult job believing the general would stoop to something so...so far reaching. But I *do* know they do radical experiments in the facility in order to make the perfect warrior."

He turned his arm over—and Casey stared.

It wasn't real.

"What happened?"

"I went in with a minor injury. They put me under, cut it off, and replaced it with an artificial arm. They wanted to do more, but I refused a second operation."

"Your father is a prick," Felix said. "He needs to be stopped."

Jonathan gave a curt nod. "I'll talk to William. Neither of us will be part of any black ops team to move on you again, but I don't know how you will stop him. The general is a determined man. He always gets what he wants."

Felix smiled, and it held a smidge of nasty. "He won't this time. We'll make sure of it—because we have a plan."

Chapter Thirteen

C asey strode into the Mitchells' private shuttle and strapped in. Felix settled in the pilot's seat and started the engines.

He shot her a sidelong glance. "Are you ready for this?"

"Not really." She gave a soft laugh. "Is it that obvious?"

"I know how I'd feel in your position. You haven't changed your mind?"

"No. The general needs to be stopped, and I have the power to do it. It's obvious he doesn't care who he harms." Her stomach quivered at the thought of confronting the general in his lair.

Felix reached for her hand and squeezed. "I'll be with you every step of the way. You won't be alone with him at any time."

"Promise?"

"You're my wife. I won't let anything happen to you."

"General, Captain Seonaid is here to see you." His aide poked his head through the door. "Do you want to see her now?"

"Show her in." General Seonaid leaned back in his chair and allowed himself a smug smile. He'd known she'd come around. He'd expected her to be delivered to the medical facility, but obviously the black ops team had come through. Ah, life was good.

His office door opened, and his daughter strolled into the room. Instead of her uniform, she was wearing a dress.

A damn *dress*, in some floaty material, and...*phrullin'* gods...was that makeup?

A tall, dark-haired man, fit and military material, ambled after her. They both halted in front of his desk. Although curious about the man's identity, he was more interested in his rebellious daughter. At last, greatness was within his grasp. Now that his daughter was here, she was within his power. He had soldiers at his disposal.

She wouldn't get away again.

His gaze narrowed when she stared at him in a direct manner, and her lack of respect raised his ire. "Soldiers don't salute any longer?"

"I'm not in the military. *You* organized that."

Low-level anger pulsed in his chest. "Saluting is a show of respect."

Her chin lifted in defiance, and challenge glinted in her eyes. "I don't respect you."

Anger swarmed like insects, attacking his brain, attacking his pride, attacking his control. "The medical facility is awaiting your arrival. My aide will arrange your transport."

"I don't think so," the man said.

General Seonaid shot him a hard scowl. "Who the devil are you? This is none of your business."

"This is Felix Mitchell," Casey said. "He's my husband, and we've just—"

"I'm calling the medical facility." He cut off his daughter. He didn't give a *fodo* crap what his daughter said. "Telling them you're on your way."

His daughter darted forward and snatched his communicator before he could attempt to make the call. She tossed it to the dark-haired man, who ground it beneath his heavy boot.

General Seonaid gaped at his daughter. What the hell? How dare she?

The man—Mitchell—went to the door, opened it, and called for his aide. "We require your help."

"General?" His aide hovered in the doorway.

"I will not be going to the medical facility, now or in the future. I am a married woman and have a new life elsewhere," Casey said.

"Don't be ridiculous," General Seonaid thundered. "I've gone to considerable trouble to arrange this and the results—the results will be *astounding*. You'll be better. Bigger. Stronger. The flawless specimen. The perfect soldier!" And he'd be famous because of his foresight, his ingenuity, his decision to take this step.

Mitchell moved with a speed that made General Seonaid blink. The man grabbed his collar and half hauled him out of his chair. The man's easy strength sent stabbings of fear and a rush of adrenaline through him.

"I'll have you up on charges!" General Seonaid wheezed through the chokehold.

"I don't think so," Mitchell said with confidence. "Sweetheart, do you have that statement we gave to the media? It's time to finish this bullshit before I end up on charges of murder for throttling your father."

Mitchell released him without warning, and General Seonaid straightened his shirt, more fear stirring...until he recalled the weapon in his drawer. And there was also a security button. Help was but a summons away.

Yeah, he could still play this game. A winning game.

Captain Seonaid pulled a piece of paper from her purse. Her purse, *phrull* it. What kind of soldier carried a purse? His bottom lip curled. After she'd shown the desire and aptitude for the military, he should have sent her to military school. He might have seen the possibilities sooner if he'd paid closer attention to her as a youngster instead of ignoring her. He wouldn't have had to deal with this *fodo* crap because she'd decided she should have a say in this matter.

"This is what will appear in the media later today." She cleared her throat and glanced at Mitchell, her gaze softening as they exchanged silent communication.

General Seonaid snarled under his breath. The man had turned her into an even bigger weakling. But not for long.

His daughter started reading.

"'My name is Casey Seonaid, and I used to be a captain in the Dalcon military. Last solar month, General Seonaid, who is also my father, arranged for my service in the military to end—unbeknownst to me. He called me to his office and informed me he'd booked me into a military medical facility. This surprised me since I am physically fit and have no need of medical attention. Upon telling the general this, I was told the operation he'd arranged was experimental. He expected me to undergo nanotechnology that would transform me from a female to a male. I do not want this surgery and have repeatedly told him so, yet he continues to put pressure on me. He believes all soldiers should be from the male sex'."

"Lies!" General Seonaid snapped. "No one will believe this drivel."

"But they will," Mitchell said. "Because we have proof of your intentions. Keep reading your statement, sweetheart."

"'When I failed to show up at the medical facility, the general authorized a black ops team to descend on the resort where I now live to retrieve me against my will. Luckily, my husband's resort has very good security, and we thwarted their mission. These soldiers, one of whom was my brother, were sent back to Dalcon with a message for my father.'

"'He ignored that message and sent another black ops team. Once again, the team failed. My other brother was part of this second extraction attempt.'

"'My brother has since revealed to me he had previously received a minor wound on his arm. A medical team put him out for surgery, and when he woke, he discovered his arm was no longer flesh and blood but machinery. The medical facility conducted cyber technology without his permission. They performed the unnecessary operation on the order of my father, General Seonaid'."

"That's not true."

"Shut up," Mitchell snapped. "Let her finish."

"'We have discovered from a source at the medical facility that General Seonaid has authorized several operations to test technology on other soldiers. This must stop. It is an abuse of power, and it is wrong for anyone to hold that sort of power over others. I submit General Seonaid be tried by the military courts for his crimes, be stripped of his rank, and be dishonorably discharged.'

"'Casey Seonaid'."

"No one will believe a word you say."

"They already do. Jonathan has also given a statement to the media. The story should be hitting the streets in..." She glanced at her wrist unit. "Oh—now."

Traces of panic tingled in his belly. No. This wasn't happening. He wouldn't believe it. *Fodo* crap, no one would believe the words of a mere woman! "You can't do this."

Heavy footsteps sounded in the outer office, and he almost sighed in relief.

"That will be the black ops team to escort you to the medical facility. Believe me—you'll thank me once the operation is complete. You'll be a better soldier," he declared, desperate to regain control of the situation. "And I've sent a team to retrieve that meddling bitch Elsa. You'll go to the facility if you know what's good for your aunt," he said smugly.

His daughter stalked toward his desk, fury twisting her face. "Not in this lifetime, *Daddy dearest*. And black ops don't work for you anymore."

Without warning, she slapped him across the face. The sharp sting rocked him back while shock bloomed to the tune of the sound.

"That is assault!" General Seonaid spat. He cupped his cheek, and his fingers came away with blood, his flesh scratched by her nails. "I'll have your head for this!"

Casey stared at the general's contorted face. He wasn't mentally stable. He couldn't be if he expected to use his children as medical experiments. And she'd bet that was just the stuff they knew about. He'd probably stomped over many soldiers on his way to the top.

Fiercely glad at the way they'd cut him off at the knees—even if he didn't yet realize the extent of the actions they'd taken—she stared at the man who was her father.

He still thought he could wriggle free of his troubles. She could see it on his face. He didn't understand this was the end. With her statement, her brother's statement, and an ambitious investigative reporter on the case, his prized promotion would explode in his face. By the time the reporter finished with him, the general wouldn't have much of his precious reputation left.

But the worst thing was Casey didn't feel a scrap of pity for him. She felt for her brother and the general's other victims. But the general—she wouldn't have any trouble turning her back and walking away. Felix's family had shown her more love than she'd ever had in her lifetime. And with Aunt Elsa setting up shop at the resort, life couldn't get much better.

Although everything had happened so quickly, she loved Felix with a fierceness that stole her breath whenever she looked at him. Their life would only get better.

Several soldiers entered the general's office. They fanned out, eyes watchful and weapons at the ready.

"Arrest her! Take her straight to the medical facility and report back once she is under lock and key," the general ordered.

"I don't think so." General Gallagher filled the doorway. "Arrest General Seonaid. Take him to lockdown."

Casey watched her father, saw the punch of shock on his face—and just a sliver of cunning as his agile mind attempted a way to spin this situation. The general stood and the solar light streaming through the windows struck the gold braid on his uniform.

"What are the charges?" he demanded.

"Atrocities against those under your command and abuse of position, for a start," General Gallagher said in an even voice.

"Where is the proof?"

"We have proof," General Gallagher said with distaste. "Take him away."

The soldiers advanced on him, and the general made his move.

Casey had expected it. He was a proud man, an arrogant man, and getting led away by underlings would not suit him.

Casey slid her weapon from the side pocket of her dress. She'd previously set it to stun—and fired before the general's own weapon cleared his desk drawer.

He dropped to the floor, a look of surprise frozen on his face.

"I bet that felt good, sweetheart." Felix moved to her side and took the weapon from her.

The soldiers secured the general and carried the unconscious man from his office.

"How did you know he'd grab a weapon?" General Gallagher

asked. "I assumed he'd do the dignified thing when faced with armed soldiers."

"His pride in his position is colossal. His arrogance is almost as large. When he comes to and when he's faced with the charges, he'll still assert his innocence and try to blame someone else," Casey said. "I know how his mind works."

"You should have come to me earlier," General Gallagher said, his stern face softening when Felix wrapped his arm around her waist.

"You wouldn't have believed me."

The general gave a heavy sigh. "No, you're right."

"He's covered his tracks well and used fear to keep everyone in line. If I hadn't confronted my brothers, hadn't learned about Jonathan's arm, others mightn't have believed me."

"This is gonna be a *fodo* crap storm," the general muttered and rubbed his hand over his face. "There will be other soldiers out there... Gods!"

"I suspect my mother has been modified," Casey said. "She might know of others if you can't get information out of the medical facility staff. But I believe they'll cooperate. Contact Dr. Phillips."

"Your mother?" Horror laced the general's voice.

"I'm afraid so. William doesn't know how lucky he was because he would've been next." Casey made a mental note to contact her mother. Maybe things would be different between them now that the general was out of the way. Or maybe not, but she had to give her mother a chance.

Yes, she thought, and she felt good about that decision. As soon as things settled down, she'd approach her mother and see how the meeting panned out before taking the next step.

"Do you need us for anything else, General?" Felix asked.

"No, not at present," the general said, his mind obviously miles away.

"You can contact us at the resort if you need us," Casey said.

"Congratulations on your marriage."

"Thank you, sir," Casey said. "I'm a lucky woman." And that was an understatement.

Felix stared at the bolts of fabric filling most of the second room in Casey's tiny city apartment. "All of this?"

"Yes. I'll be able to use most of this fabric in designs for the boutique."

"Sweetheart, you're a pack rat."

She wrinkled her cute nose and looked baffled. "I don't know what that is, but it sounds insulting."

Felix laughed and hugged her, still unable to believe that this wonderful woman was his wife. His very feminine wife, even if she did know many ways to kill a man. "Let's get started then. What are we going to pack it in?"

"Aunt Elsa can suggest a mover company. They have machines that cover the items with a special coating to protect them."

"I don't care what it costs. Call them."

She grinned. "I'll do it now. They only need to pack and ship the stuff in this room. The rest of the stuff came with the apartment. The next tenant will inherit it." She picked up her communicator and made the call to her aunt, who'd arrived safely back at the resort just that morning.

Felix wandered out to the other room. It was dark and dingy compared to the fabric room. He doubted Casey would have any regrets leaving this hole. His com-circle squawked and he answered it absently. "Felix."

"It's Saber. Can you come to Dalcon and pick us up? I'm injured and can't pilot the shuttle. You'll need to bring someone to fly back my shuttle."

"How badly are you injured?"

"Shot with a laz-weapon. Not gonna die, but I feel like crap."

"Where are you? I'm in Dalcon City now."

"At the castle." Saber paused and murmured something to someone in the background. "The king said he'll get us to the shuttle port."

The king? "When?"

"About an hour?" Saber asked.

"We'll be there."

"Who's with you?" Saber asked.

"My wife, Casey," Felix said with a grin. "She can pilot the other shuttle back to Ione."

"A wife... Sounds as if we both have stories to tell. Catch ya soon, bro."

"All sorted," Casey said. "Someone is coming straight over. Aunt Elsa said they were efficient."

"Slight change of plans. Saber has been injured and needs us to fly him home. Can you pilot our other shuttle back to the resort? We need to meet Saber in an hour at the port."

"Sure. Let me pack up a few things to get me started." She darted into the other room, and Felix heard her muttering and the thump of various items.

Casey was true to her word, and a short time later, they caught an air-glide to the shuttle port.

"Eva!" Casey cried and was off like a rabbit.

Felix spotted Saber standing beside Eva. His face was pale, but he was standing on two feet. "Hey," he said. "Let's get you on the shuttle."

"Sir, which shuttle is yours?" a large man asked. He was beefy with red skin. Even his thick black hair bore a red tinge. "The king instructed us to aid you with your luggage."

"Port 3," Casey said. "Position C."

The red man nodded and spoke to his companion. In a short time they organized a cyber-porter, and the mechanical man pulled a cart bearing their luggage. The red men followed.

"Where is the other shuttle?" Casey asked. "Can Eva come with me so we can catch up?"

Felix could see the hesitation in Saber. "Eva will be safe with Casey, and we'll be following them."

Finally, Saber nodded. Once he and Felix were in their shuttle, one of the red men escorted the two women to theirs. In a short time, they were on their way home.

"How are things at the resort?" Saber asked.

"We've had problems, but I've sorted them. I kicked Laurence out. He was the one who was cutting the fence. We caught him cutting another hole *and* feeding the zylon."

"Fuck," Saber muttered.

"He blames our family for Lori's death," Felix said. "He's not trustworthy, and it's better now that he's gone. The rest of the employees seem more settled, so I think he's been stirring resentment behind the scenes."

"Good job," Saber said. "I had my suspicions but wasn't sure how to prove them."

"We put a silent alarm on the fence. It's saved our butts a couple of times." And he told Saber about the visits from the amphibious tribe, plus the black ops.

"You sound happy for someone who's been so busy," Saber said.

"I am. I'm crazy about Casey. Ma, Casey, and Casey's aunt Elsa are starting a boutique. It's going to create jobs for some of the women and more revenue."

"Eva is setting up a restaurant at the resort, and maybe something on a smaller scale in the employee village," Saber said. "It happened quickly, but I love her. Even more than I loved Lori."

Felix reached over and squeezed Saber's shoulder. "I know the feeling. How bad is your injury? Do we need to worry?"

"It's healing, but the king's physician said it will take time."

"Ma will make sure you rest."

Saber gave a wry smile. "So will Eva."

"You don't need to worry about the resort. Everything is going great. We've planted the grapes, and they're doing well. Joe and Sly are pleased with the vines. The zylon population seems under control."

"Sounds good. I promised Eva we could laze on the beach and relax while we thought about our plans."

"You'll have to get past Ma first. She was pissed when Casey and I got married so quickly. She's planning a party."

"So if I tell her that Eva and I are getting married too, she'll be in her element," Saber said.

"Out of our hair," Felix said and laughed. "Good plan."

The lunar-moon sent a delicate light over the party while a series of colored lamps shed both illumination and shadows. Casey slow-danced with Felix, something she'd never done before and couldn't work out why. The feel of his muscular arms around her brought a sense of security to battle other, more lustful thoughts. Somehow, she'd grabbed the perfect man, found the one who completed her, and she couldn't imagine feeling happier. Giddy euphoria bubbled inside her, and she pressed closer to her husband.

On the other side of the party, Eva sat with Saber. Their heads were close together, and their fingers were twined. She'd never seen Eva like this before either, and that made joy swell within her heart. Now she had friends as well as a husband, and a new job to fulfill her creative side.

"I love you, Felix," Casey said.

Felix stopped swaying and pulled away, enough to glimpse her face. His breath caught at whatever he saw, and he tugged her away from the other dancers. "We're leaving," he said in a gruff voice.

"But we should say good night to everyone," she protested.

"We're on our honeymoon. They need to get used to us disappearing."

"But they'll know what we're doing."

He smirked. "Newsflash, sweetheart. They can smell you all over my skin and me on yours. They already know we're married and can connect the dots."

Casey felt heat bloom in her cheeks nonetheless.

Felix pressed his palm on their suite door and dragged her inside. Once the door locked behind them, he turned to her, his green eyes glowing in the catlike way that spoke of great emotion.

Her hands went to the lace fastenings on the side of her dress. Without breaking their connection, she wriggled out of her dress to reveal the silky bit of nothing she wore beneath.

"You're so beautiful, Casey. I have never felt happier."

She kicked off her *Elsa Sparkle* shoes and reached for his hand. "Let's celebrate this love of ours, husband."

"I like that word on your lips."

Casey grinned and unbuttoned his shirt. She tossed it aside and went to work on his trousers. With one quick yank, his trousers and underwear slid down his legs.

"Shoes?" he asked with laughter in his voice.

"Smartass." She kneeled to work off his shoes, then craving the taste of him, rose a fraction to give his cock some attention. She sucked him deep into her mouth, felt the quick jolt go through his body, and wanted to chuckle. She teased him, licked, and took him deep, massaging his crown with the flat of her tongue.

Finally, she pulled back. "I want you inside me."

"Yes."

She led him to their sleep-bed, and looked at him, puzzled, when he resisted her push to the bed.

"I want a kiss."

"Whenever you like." Casey tipped up her head. "I do love you."

"Pleased to hear it." And he took her lips, hard and sure. She clung, opening her mouth to him, tangling their tongues together in a kiss so intimate, so special, so thrilling that her toes curled. Each time he touched her, it was like a blow to her heart. Her pulse rate sped, and her body moistened. Even now, it was difficult to believe they were married and would remain together forever. In good times and in bad, she thought. *Always.*

He scooped her off her feet and placed her on the sleep-bed. His eyes traced the curves of her body, the lean lines of her, and dwelled on her lacy underwear. "These are pretty, but they have to go."

In seconds flat, she was naked. He kissed her jaw, her neck and headed straight for the tiny tattoo at the place where neck and shoulder joined. His lips surrounded it, sucked, and sensations cut through her like a laser knife. A moan sounded, and she realized the throaty noise came from her. His tongue teased the spot before he moved down her body, giving each of his favorite parts special attention. He had a lot of favorites, and by the time he parted her legs, she wanted to beg him to hurry.

Felix lifted her to his mouth and did some precision work on her clit. Her hands gripped his hair and tugged.

"Ow, woman. Are you trying to scalp me?"

A giggle—yes, a giggle—erupted from her as he grinned in return.

He moved over her and thrust inside with one perfect stroke. He filled her with joy, with sensual expectation, with his cock, and it felt oh so good.

Perfect.

Felix didn't hurry. He stroked into her almost lazily but glided to the hilt each time. Pleasure unfurled like a flower blooming from a bud. The sensations grew and expanded, became better.

"Felix," she cried. "I love you."

"Love you too, sweetheart." He thrust again, and this time, she exploded, taking him with her. They rode out the swells of passion together as lovers. Husband and wife.

Felix withdrew and gathered her against his hard frame. "I liked you from the moment I saw you."

"You did?"

"I did," he confirmed. "And now that I've captured you, you're not getting free."

"Works for me," Casey said and kissed him. This is what happiness felt like, she thought in wonder. She liked this feeling.

He gathered her even closer if that was possible. And they spent the rest of the night making love.

Fast.

Slow.

And in between.

It was very, very good.

Would you like to read more of my romances? Sign up for my newsletter https://shelleymunro.com/newsletter/ to learn about upcoming releases, receive free books and short stories tied to my series plus contest and special promotion news.

Please turn the page to glimpse *Lost with Leo*, book three in the Middlemarch Capture series.

EXCERPT – LOST WITH LEO

The Dalcon spaceport was crazy busy. Leo Mitchell scanned the crowds of locals and alien tourists who thronged the arrival hall and toyed with the idea of hitting someone. Perhaps one of the big red dudes with swirling tentacles around their heads. Their meaty fists looked as if they could do some damage. If he was injured or unconscious he'd have a good excuse to miss his appointment.

Leo pondered his scheme and dragged his hand through his hair, pausing as his fingers met a hat. Oh yeah. He'd shaved off his long locks. Scowling, he straightened his cap.

Hell. This picking a fight was looking better and better. *How hard would they hit?* A black eye, a wired jaw, a plethora of bruises decorating his body. He imagined the repercussions and his shoulders slumped. He had to keep his word because he needed the final payment to get the farming side of their enterprise fully operational.

No alternative.

Leo hefted a backpack over one shoulder and navigated a path through the mass of travelers. He circled the Red Mumber males despite the urge to lash out and punch them in their muscled midriffs. Innocents. They didn't deserve his problems heaped on their heads, not after he'd walked into the trap under his own steam.

Beware of petite women bearing gifts.

His mouth twisted as he dodged two upright aliens with pale-blue skin. That was one gift horse he should've punched in the mouth. Worse, he'd fucked her in his dreams last night, spanked her pert arse because she hadn't focused on him.

Weird.

He wanted to hate her—hell, most of the time, he did detest her—but in his dreams, he fucked her and enjoyed the experience. All kinds of messed up. A shrink would have a fun party with that screwed-up scenario.

He sidestepped a kid—at least, he thought it was a child—as the hard-shelled creature scuttled past on all fours. One last meeting. All he had to do was endure this last session with Iseult Orna, collect her money, and head back to the resort, a man free of obligations.

One final session.

Leo sucked in a deep breath and exited the arrival hall.

Makeshift stalls bordered the streets and created jams in the pedestrian areas. Fly-scoots darted overhead, avoiding the hordes of people but facing problems of their own as they jockeyed for airspace on their journey through the city. Market day was profitable for some, but it made for volatile crowds and short tempers.

Up ahead, the crowd jostled a stooped and wizened woman. Several Tigrus youths, recognizable by their striped skin, hooted with laughter as the woman's shopping flew through the air. Bright-pink fruits spilled from a bag and rolled along the rutted cobblestones. A jar of liquid struck the ground and shattered in an explosion of white.

Leo glared in the youths' direction and stooped to pick up as many of the woman's possessions as possible. "Here you go, ma'am. How far are you going?"

Up close, the woman was even older than he'd thought. Her face was a mass of lines, and she had one large milky eye instead of two like him. It blinked as she regarded him. Alarm jerked in him, a wince in reaction, and he broke their gaze. That was plain creepy.

"To the corner," she wheezed. "My shop is there."

"Let me carry your shopping for you," Leo said.

"Thank ye." Her bony hand fastened around his arm, and he fought to maintain a pleasant expression. She not only looked and sounded old, but she smelled ancient—a combination of dirt and moldy leaves with a hint of green to freshen her scent and push it a tad above disgusting.

She leaned on him and moved at a snail's pace in ponderous steps. The journey to her shop stretched along with his disquiet. He unlocked the door and helped her inside. The building appeared dingy from the outside but bore a clean and ordered interior. Much bigger and cavernous than he'd expected. Herbs and dried flowers hung from hooks and perfumed the space. Transparent boxes and jars held things foreign and creepy. His attention snagged on one. Were those dried fingers?

"Thank ye," she said again. "Can I offer you refreshments?"

"No, I'm fine. I was glad to help you, but I have an appointment." Leo turned away, unease pushing him to haste.

"Wait." The woman's hand shot out, and she gripped Leo's arm, her fingernails digging into his flesh. "Let me give you some advice."

"Advice?" Leo's skin crawled, and he had to force himself not to bolt.

Her gaze bored into him, equally horrifying and magnetic. *Scary as hell.* "Today will be hard, boy, but you will live where others have died."

Leo's stomach bucked, the remnants of his coffee and chocolate roll eaten at the resort sloshing in an alarming manner and threatening to charge up his throat. How could she know what he intended to do today? What was expected of him? "I don't know what you mean."

Bright red swirled into her eye, combined with the white, and bled into pale pink. "Listen to me, boy. You will survive. Don't let revenge blacken your heart and make you so blind you can't accept what is in front of you." Her fingers tightened on his arm. "Remember what I say, boy. Don't let revenge take you over. Now let me give you some tonic. No charge," she added before he could argue.

Leo nodded even as his mind tried to reject her words.

She hobbled over to a shelf, appeared to ponder her choice, then reached for a glass vial. After pausing again, she reached for a second. "This will help you recover. Drink entire vial. One now. One after." She pulled out a stopper and handed the glass vessel to him. "Drink," she urged.

Leo scrutinized the vial then figured *what the hell.* God, the liquid smelled revolting. He glanced at the woman and she gave a small nod of encouragement.

She wasn't going to let him escape without drinking the stuff. He took a quick breath and gulped the contents. His stomach pitched and roiled, and he swallowed urgently to keep down the tonic.

"Good. Good." She cackled, displaying a gap in her bottom set of teeth in her amusement. "Put other in jacket pocket. Drink after."

Sharp teeth, he noted, and shuddered as he stuffed the vial in his pocket. Some of these alien types were freaky. "Thank you. I'd better go or I'll be late for my appointment."

"Thank ye, boy, for a kindness to an old lady."

"You're welcome," Leo said with the manners ingrained by his parents, and with a last polite smile, he stalked from the shop. His rapid breaths evened out as he stepped into the street to merge with the market crowd. The semi-fresh air helped to settle the rocking and rolling in the pit of his stomach. Instead, a strange warmth filled him. Peculiar, but not unpleasant. He continued to his destination.

Iseult Orna lived in the better part of the city, near the palace. Her mansion stood at the end of a cul-de-sac with no near neighbors. A tall stone fence kept unwanted visitors out, the razor wire running along the top and security guards punctuating her preference for privacy.

The closer he came to the palace, the harder he needed to work to force his limbs to function.

Fear.

It was a tight band around his chest, restricting his breathing until it felt as if each breath emerged and entered through a straw.

The mansion came into sight, and each inhalation sawed into his lungs. He forced his tense limbs to carry him to the gates, to ring the bell for entrance. A voice squawked from a concealed speaker, and Leo backed away in quick, jerky steps, the flight response kicking in big time.

Run. Run. *Run!*

Yet his promise to honor a contract kept his feet firm, and he stated his business in a steady voice. "Leo Mitchell to see Iseult Orna."

The gates bearing the crest of a spider parted and slid back with nary a sound to allow him entrance to Spiderus Mansion. Leo strode up the driveway, past the gardens, to where a petite woman waited for him. A brown mouse with brown hair, brown eyes and a secretive nature. She looked as if she wasn't capable of spitting at a fly, let alone hurting one.

He knew better.

A snarl rumbled up his throat, and if he could've shot flames with his eyes, she'd be burning in hell.

Betrys Torin.

She was the traitorous bitch who'd lured him into this trap with her timid yet persuasive ways. His hands clenched at his sides. Weird, but she was also the sexy siren whom he'd fucked in his dreams. Confusion about the way his brain fired lately was an understatement. He loathed Betrys for getting him into this situation with Iseult Orna, yet during his dreams last night, he and Betrys had rolled around together naked, did decadent things to each other...

He shook himself, squared his shoulders, and took a deep breath as if preparing for battle. In a sense, this was war.

Sure, Iseult Orna was beautiful, but her heart was as black as her hair, and her sexual predilections were far from normal.

He'd been cocky during their first meeting, a little arrogant, but Iseult had soon slapped the swagger out of him. Shocked, traumatized after their first fucking, he'd tried to backtrack and renege on the deal.

Iseult, backed up by her muscle men, had disabused him of the notion, so he'd turned up for the second fucking and healthy payment. A fine tremor went through Leo, even though he struggled to maintain an impassive façade. The second encounter with Iseult had been even worse.

This third and final session might just kill him.

Purchase Lost With Leo today
https://shelleymunro.com/books/lost-with-leo/

ALSO BY SHELLEY

Middlemarch Shifters
My Scarlet Woman
My Younger Lover
My Peeping Tom
My Assassin
My Estranged Lover
My Feline Protector
My Determined Suitor
My Cat Burglar
My Stray Cat
My Second Chance
My Plan B
My Cat Nap
My Romantic Tangle
My Blue Lady
My Twin Trouble
My Precious Gift
My Grumpy Wolf

Middlemarch Gathering
My Highland Mate
My Highland Fling
My Elusive Mate
My Valiant Princess
My Highland Wedding
My Highland Billionaire

Middlemarch Capture
Snared by Saber
Favored by Felix
Lost with Leo
Spellbound with Sly
Journey with Joe
Star-Crossed with Scarlett

House of the Cat
Captured & Seduced
Claimed & Seduced
Merry & Seduced
Stranded & Seduced
Seized & Seduced
Hunted & Seduced
Festive & Seduced
Betrayed & Seduced
Enticed & Seduced

Dragon Investigators
Blue Moon Dragon
Blood Moon Dragon
Black Moon Dragon
Snow Moon Dragon

About Shelley

USA Today bestselling author Shelley Munro lives in Auckland, the City of Sails, with her husband and a cheeky Jack Russell/mystery breed dog.

Typical New Zealanders, Shelley and her husband left home for their big OE soon after they married (translation of New Zealand speak - big overseas experience). A twelve-month-long adventure lengthened to six years of roaming the world. Enduring memories include being almost sat on by a mountain gorilla in Rwanda, lazing on white sandy beaches in India, whale watching in Alaska, searching for leprechauns in Ireland, and dealing with ghosts in an English pub.

While travel is still a big attraction, these days Shelley is most likely found in front of her computer following another love - that of writing stories of contemporary and paranormal romance and adventure. Other interests include watching rugby (strictly for research purposes), cycling, playing croquet and the ukelele, and curling up with an enjoyable book.

Visit Shelley at her Website
https://shelleymunro.com

Join Shelley's Newsletter
https://shelleymunro.com/newsletter